WILD DEVIL

SINNERS & SAINTS
BOOK 3

LANA SKY

Wild Devil

Wild Devil By Lana Sky

Cover Design and Interior Formatting by Charity Chimni
Editing by Charity Chimni
Alpha Reading by Jessica Rita Rampersad

ACKNOWLEDGMENTS

Thanks so much to everyone who supported this draft along the way, including the many beta readers who provided encouragement! Please keep in mind that this story includes dark, graphic, and explicit content matter that may not be suitable for readers under the age of 18—or for readers who are uncomfortable with the following subject matter: drug use, mentions of suicide, cultish behavior, explicit sex, and graphic depictions of violence.

ONE

DAZE

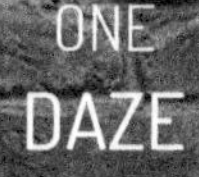

"CALM DOWN, DAZE," Ben snaps at me from across a narrow room.

Actually, it's more like a crude concrete square, surrounded by plywood nailed to a shoddy frame. The cartel once used it as a logistics center for storing and transporting stolen car parts, according to Marco—one of the few who stayed behind. It's no five-star hotel, that's for damn sure. The structure is drafty as hell, and every sound echoes. It is, however, easily defendable, and large enough to serve as a base.

Besides, beggars can't be choosers, and it's just about the only safe place in Westpoint City.

"You'll give yourself a heart attack before Silas or Heywood can put a bullet through it first," my second-in-command continues. "Have a seat."

The request seems to be purely symbolic, considering there aren't even any chairs around—not that I care. I keep pacing, slamming one foot in front of the other as I try to think. "I can't just sit on my ass while Frey is still in there," I say out loud. My voice is so gruff I can hardly recognize it.

"Take a breath, at least," Ben calls out. "Look, I know your girl is in danger, but you're just torturing yourself at this point. Slow down."

Danger is putting it lightly. Every minute she's in the hands of those monsters, her life is at risk. Because of me.

Though, I wouldn't put it past Ben to knock me the fuck out to keep me from going to her, if he had to.

Besides, we haven't been twiddling our thumbs. Damien and his boys, along with any stragglers Ben could gather, met us after Frey left. Here, our team has begun to reorganize, coming up with a plan to take down Heywood and Silas once and for all.

So far, it goes something like this—keep an eye on the church.

Recruit a capable crew of allies.

Try not to go fucking insane in the meantime.

Surprise, that last part is the most difficult. My sanity went with Frey as she skipped into the enemy's lair alone. The old Daze Keaton would never admit as much, but her absence feels unnatural—like a part of my body is missing. An arm. A leg. A piece of my damn soul. Whatever it is, I can't function for long without it.

Without *her.*

"Any news?" I ask Ben for the umpteenth time.

"No, Daze, things haven't magically changed in the last five minutes since you asked." Rolling his eyes, Ben crosses his arms. "Lyra took Sam home, despite us telling her to stick around here. Don't worry, I'll keep an eye on her. As for your girl, she's still at the church, and Kane is there, making sure we know the second she's moved. Damien's out trying to track down that reporter guy, and Lex is getting specialized computer equipment—"

"The point is, they're all being useful," I grit out, eyeing my hands. They're bruised and scraped to hell and back. Even so, I can imagine feeling her warm, soft skin so damn clearly it stings. My fingers flex as if to hold the sensation, but it disappears within seconds.

"Day—" Ben doesn't bother to hide his worry as I look up. "Sit down," he says.

Still pacing, I let my hands fall to my sides. "Tell me again why I'm waiting around here? I should be out there."

"Because you'd be shot to pieces on sight should you go gallivanting around the city. According to Kane, the security at the church is so tight, he can't even get close. The men Silas has on patrol are probably looking for you, and they won't just crack open your skull like before. You'll be killed on sight, and then what about Frey?"

"Heywood was always going to have her locked down tight," I counter, thinking out loud. Maybe this—the millionth time I've gone over this scenario—will be the one time I finally discover a breakthrough. "All I'd have to do is cause a distraction and we take out as many of the guards as we can."

Ben sighs. "We went over this, Day. You need to fight this war on two fronts. Two separate strategies. Besides, what do you really think will happen if you barge in to play the hero? They'll just let you walk out with her?"

"Maybe I should go find out?" I can't resist the temptation any longer. Curling my hands into fists, I make my way toward the battered metal doors at the front of the warehouse, a few paces from our makeshift command center.

"Oh, come on! Not this again. Look at me." Ben rushes forward to grab my shoulders with lightning speed. "Read my lips, Day. You. Can't. Save. Her. *Yet—*"

"I know." I push away from him, tearing my hands through my hair. "I know..." The anger is all for show. Once again, he's right. I need to clear my mind and strategize if Frey has any chance. It's what she'd urge me to do—instead of thinking with my dick, think like a fucking leader.

After all, she supposedly gave me the blueprint to take down Michael Heywood. I cast a glance over my shoulder and wince. Everything she left for me to find is scattered over a ratty metal table, including a tablet, a business card, a journal, and her final message—*Trust me. Hale tried to tell me the truth, and I owe it to him to get him justice. Don't come after me yet—I'll come to you. I can handle myself. After all, I learned from the best. —Love, Frey.*

She put more trust in me than I deserve, because what have I learned since then? Fucking nada.

"Lex's working on cracking the info on that tablet," Ben insists. "He'll come up with something soon. You just gotta be patient. You know how long that tech-shit can take—"

"Knowing what Frey does, how long do you think they'll keep her around? The bastard's already killed one of his children." And I may have failed Hale, but I refuse to lose Frey. "We need to be proactive."

"We are. I'm almost done going through the journal. See?" Snatching the item from the table, he brandishes it in a fist. "All we need is to find this Jamie Colland guy—"

"For a reporter, he's a tricky motherfucker to pin down," a different voice cuts in.

I whirl around. As if he appeared from thin air, a six-foot-tall figure leans against the wall in a corner of the warehouse, arms crossed, green eyes watchful. "I couldn't even get a visual on him," he adds with a shrug. "Looks like he's gone dark on all of his socials, too."

"When the fuck did you get back, Damien?" I ask him, but that's not important. "How is Frey? Has Kane seen her?"

"Easy with the twenty questions! I didn't learn much." He throws up his hands in surrender, but his cocky grin reveals he hasn't come up entirely short. "I tracked down his address, but he isn't there—and it's not hard to figure out why. His place is being surveilled by the Saints. Looks like we aren't the only ones interested in what he has to say."

I grit my teeth. "Ah, fuck. We need to find him." If Silas is on the same trail, that task just got ten times harder.

"Your girl keeps strange company," Damien adds, his expression unreadable.

I raise an eyebrow. "What do you mean?"

"Kane says she's got at least six guards on her, but they seem on edge—more than they should be. It reminded him of the setup for an ambush, but you know how it is—you do one tour too many in the Middle East, and suddenly everyone's a suicide bomber—"

"What the fuck is that supposed to mean?" I ask. The worst potential reasons are already dancing across my mind.

She will be killed before this is over.

"Don't shoot the messenger." Damien smirks. The threat of violence excites the motherfucker—even if it's at my expense. Then he frowns and cocks his head, suddenly serious. "His concern makes sense. Heywood's only visited her once before scurrying back to that mansion. Why not keep her there? Unless it's the ol' bait and switch. Distract your enemy with a smokescreen, while concealing your true aim within the chaos. Kane would guess an I.E.D., but I'm sure this Heywood fellow would go for something a little more subtle than that—"

"Like Frey," Ben insists with a know-it-all frown. "*She's* the distraction. You get sidetracked now, and you might as well slit your own throat, Day. Tell me you can't see that."

"You might have a point," I admit, hating my own words. This sounds like defeat, a hopeless admission that I can't get her back. Or maybe it's the first fucking coherent thought I've had all day. "Let's say she *is* a decoy." I turn around in time to see Ben's reaction.

Slowly, he nods along as if following the same train of thought. "Alright. Keep talking."

What else would I do in Heywood's shoes? It doesn't take a genius to figure out the obvious answer.

"If I were him, that's the only reason why I'd keep her at the church," I spit out. "As a decoy. The real question to ask is what he *doesn't* want me to see. What are we missing?"

Ben strokes his chin without offering up an answer.

"Why don't we swing by that mansion?" Damien suggests, his lips quirked. Damn. I know that look—he's up to something.

Still, his hunch is the best one we've got. "Why?"

"Heywood doesn't strike me as the type to spend a quiet evening at home while his daughter is held captive across town," he says.

"Hmm." Ben continues to stroke his chin. Then he jerks his head toward me. "Why does he even give a shit about you anyway? You're a fly in his orbit. He can't fear some crazy ex-gangbanger with no real crew or territory to back him up."

"Jesus, Ben, enough with the compliments," I say with a scoff. "I might get a bigger ego than I already have."

"Hey! I'm just playing along. It's your job to answer my questions. So, tell me why."

"Let's hear it, Day," Damien rests his head against the wall, his gaze shrouded in shadow. "What could be more important to the bastard than winning the election or punishing his pretty, disobedient daughter?"

My eyes narrow at the offhand compliment, but I focus on the task at hand first. "Something must be going down soon," I surmise. "Something he can't risk putting off. Maybe a meeting with Silas? Or even the cartel. If I were him, I'd think I'd be too busy trying to play hero to give a damn about anything else."

"Alright." Ben rakes a hand through his dark hair, highlighting the purple bruises beneath his eyes. I'm sure I look just as wrecked. He hasn't slept since yesterday morning, but like a true ride-or-die, he's here when I need him most. "We should check with your cartel contact. Ask if anything unusual has been happening. I know they keep tabs on the docks where their merchandise comes in. Maybe they've seen something?"

"For that information, they'll probably want something in return," Damien pitches in. "Wouldn't it be easier to just attack the church on our own and call it a day?"

I'm sure as hell down with that plan of action, or I would have been... Before Frey. No longer am I the only one in the arena, watching my own back. I have a crew to lead now.

And a real leader doesn't do shit without putting the safety of his men first. Samuel, Damien, and his boys, even the cartel holdouts...

They're all in my corner.

"We'll regroup," I say, going along with Ben's original plan. "You and I will watch the house. Kane will watch over Frey."

"She'll be fine for the night," Ben says. "I'm sure of it."

A bitter thought creeps in before I can help it—maybe she wanted it this way. Maybe this was a setup from the beginning, meant to catch me off guard. A sleeping-with-the-enemy-type deal. All along, she could have been playing me for the fool.

The thought doesn't fully enter my mind before I quash it. *Bullshit.* Frey isn't like that. If anyone would have had an ulterior motive, it's me. I'm the one who lied to her from the start and dragged her into this mess. I'm the one who failed not only her, but her brother.

I'm the monster in this fucked-up fairy tale.

"Hey." I sense Ben come up beside me before he even places his hand on my shoulder. "You're in your head again," he points out. "Tell me what you're thinking."

"Maybe going to the house is the real trap?" Turning on my heel, I start pacing all over again. "Who knows what they're doing to her in that fucking church? Leaving her there could be exactly what they want me to do."

"I doubt it," Damien pipes up. "Now, quit your bitching and tell us what to do."

I stop short and face him again. He's right. In this situation, I'm not in control, and the only option I have left is one that scares me to death.

I have to trust Frey and myself.

"Kane could be right," I admit. "We should look into Heywood's activities away from the church. Lie low. The three of us will check out the mansion and see what's going on. And in the meantime—"

"Lex will keep cracking at the tablet," Damien cuts in. "One of his government contacts is bringing in some high-tech computer equipment. In a few hours, he'll be able to tell us everything we need. Kane will stick around the church. If anything changes, you'll be the first to know."

"We'll get to the bottom of this mess," Ben says, nodding in agreement. "So, when do you want to get this shit show underway?"

I look out of a nearby, partially-boarded-up window. Through slits in the plywood, the sky is already darkening to an inky blue as night falls. A sinking feeling in my gut warns me that unless Frey is freed soon, she might never be.

But if I don't find a way to take down her father, she wouldn't accept me as her "savior" anyway.

"Now," I say to Ben. "Let's move out."

"You sure you don't want to shower first?" He casts a wary glance at my filthy sweats and tattered shirt. I haven't changed since she left. A day ago, already? It feels like a goddamn eternity.

"No." Cracking my knuckles, I turn toward the door. "We need to leave now before I change my mind."

"Yo, blondie. Hold up." My attention is drawn to the far corner of the warehouse, where shadows obscure anyone on that end. A lone man is heading my way, an eyebrow raised. He's kept mostly out of sight since we've been here, but I recognize him instantly—Marco, one of the cartel holdouts. "We need to talk first," he says, coming to a stop paces away from me. "Or are you all too busy with this pow-wow sesh?"

"I'll go get a van ready and make sure we have some backup," Ben grumbles, heading for the battered metal doors that mark the exit.

As he leaves, I size up the man standing before me. He's tall, with dark hair and enough muscle to suggest he can hold his own in a fight. I can't tell much from his guarded expression. For all I know, he could have a knife at the ready, primed to stab me in the back.

It wouldn't be the first time I trusted the wrong person.

"I want to make it clear that we aren't here to play Girl Scouts," he says once Ben is out of earshot. "You made an offer we couldn't refuse, but we aren't dogs you can keep on a leash. Don't forget our deal."

As if I could. I grind my teeth, recalling exactly what that agreement entailed—I would help them drive Silas and Heywood's goons from the city once and for all. After that? We'd go our separate ways, supposedly without any further bloodshed. How did that one saying go? The enemy of my enemy is my friend.

"So, is this your way of saying to watch my back?" I counter, keeping my tone neutral.

He shrugs. "This is my way of telling you that our loyalties still lie where they lie. But if you need any intel regarding Cortez or the other leaders, we're here to offer it. No more. No less. *Comprende?*"

I nod. "And I'm sure that you'll offer all this help in exchange for nothing. Out of the goodness of your heart, of course."

He winks. "You can bet your ass on that."

"Maybe I will."

Before this deal with the devil is all said and done, I might come to regret it.

But hell, who knows what role I'll actually play in the long run.

The cartel might have made a mistake in trusting *me*.

For the time being, I can't be too picky when it comes to allies. Hell, I can't be picky at all. "You mind if I take you up on that offer now?" I wonder out loud, my head cocked, hands at my sides.

Marco chuckles, his gaze wary but curious. "How so?"

"We're going on a little field trip," I say, nodding my head in the direction Ben went. "If you mean what you said, then come along."

After all, if anyone could know what Heywood might be up

to, it would be the very organization that created the infrastructure he's using now.

Marco purses his lips and runs a finger along his jaw. Then he nods. "Bet."

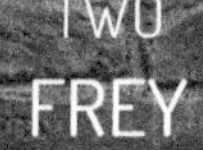

SOMETHING IS WRONG.

I haven't been dragged off to some dark, underground dungeon to be tortured. Yet. Instead, I've been locked in a windowless room near the back of the church. Father or Colton hasn't even come to gloat over me yet—and it's the lack of violence that scares me. Maybe they're hoping that Daze will come back for me first?

He would be walking into a bloodbath if he did.

God, I can only pray that he doesn't even try. Daze is brave, but violence alone isn't enough to defeat my father. To beat him at his own game, we must unravel the mysterious events in the city involving my family.

Like finding the truth behind Higher Limit Construction, an agency that has been buying up property all over Westpoint, and finally avenging my brother's death.

Nonetheless, terror starts to creep in anyway, sowing other thoughts. Were Daze and Sammy able to get away okay? What if Father had someone waiting to harm them as soon as they reunited? The cynical part of my brain eagerly rewords that statement—of course, he did.

Daze and his son could be dead, and it's all my fault.

Enough. I shake my head to snap out of the self-pitying mindset. Taking a deep breath, I clear my mind and focus, starting by straining my ears to hear the shuffling feet of a nearby guard. Then, the sounds of distant traffic warning that I'm on the far end of the building. The last guard to walk past the door to this room came an hour ago, and roughly forty-five minutes before that. How can I tell?

Because all this time, I've been counting the seconds down. *Ten. Twenty. Thirty. Sixty. Ten, Twenty. Thirty. Sixty.*

Fifty-four minutes. Sooner or later, they'll do another round, and I'll be ready. They'll knock on the door just once to check I'm still inside. Afterward, they'll give me a sandwich or a cup of whatever to tide me over. Rinse and repeat.

My hand reaches toward the hem of my dress, finding the tiny secret I hid there before leaving Ben's bar—an exposed razor blade. It's all I could locate by way of a weapon, but I don't let myself dwell on the potential risks of using it. All I need to do is think of my next plan. Keep breathing. Don't get discouraged.

Finding a way out on my own is my only option. Otherwise...

I don't want to think about it.

Instead, I wait until I finally hear footsteps approaching. Only... *Wait.* In contrast to the usual lone steps of a hired guard, two sets of steps advance toward me now. One is heavier and one distinctly lighter, as if the owner were eager to get to me. Eager to gloat. The thick cologne that Colton wears seems to fill the room before the door even opens to reveal him standing there.

The sight of his gray dress shirt and black slacks provides me some relief—he doesn't look as though he's ready for a wedding anytime soon. But what does he have in store?

As he enters the narrow space, I realize that my father isn't with him. He came here alone.

"Frances," he says, clasping his hands before him. "It breaks my heart to see you like this." His tone conveys anything but heartbreak. More like malice.

"Like what?" I counter coldly. "That I'm able to speak for myself for once?"

"No." His eyes narrow to slits, and I no longer recognize him. "Disobedient. Reveling in sin. The woman I love is modest and humble. But I have no doubt that you will return to that demeanor soon."

As he speaks, a chill runs down my spine.

"Oh?" I force myself to meet his gaze and suppress another shudder at what I see there—pure, cold emptiness. "And how do you plan on achieving that?"

"Don't be naïve, Frances." His upper lip quirks into a smirk. The expression looks out of place on him, a mocking imitation of my father's stern glare. "You will learn. In time, you will crave my touch as a wife should," he says ominously. Without warning, he advances in my direction and reaches out, swiping his fingers through my hair, ignoring how I attempt to scurry from his reach. My fingers twitch in the direction of my concealed razor—but I keep myself from drawing it.

For now.

"I have every intention of making you a woman worthy of marriage," Colton says, oblivious. "In no time at all, you will once again be the Frances we all know and love."

We? His use of that particular word makes the hair on the back of my neck go up.

"I'm sure my father will teach you everything he knows on the subject," I snipe. "I bet you're looking forward to that."

His eyebrows go up and I recognize the emotion flashing through his gaze as fear. Not because of my tone but because of what I said. I'd come close to uncovering something, but what?

"Well, he is an expert on shaping and controlling women," I add to twist the knife. "Isn't he?"

"Don't play coy." Colton draws back, his expression blank. "I think it's a good thing that our wedding will be expedited—"

"When?" My voice breaks, and I hate myself for showing even a sliver of weakness before him.

"Soon." His smirk returns. "There are arrangements that need to be made first. I know this isn't the most comfortable of accommodations…"

"It's fine." Despite only a plastic mattress for comfort and having to be escorted to the bathroom by an armed guard, I'd rather be here than anywhere near him or my father.

But I'm not naïve. They won't keep me here for long, and I need to learn as much as I can now—before it's too late.

"Wait," I call out before Colton can leave the room fully. "Why are you doing this?"

"Doing what?" He spins to face me as if he's genuinely confused by the question. "Caring about you? Wanting to save your soul from damnation?"

"No." I lick my lips and ask, "Why do you want me at all? What do you stand to gain?"

As his expressionless mask quivers once again, I know I've hit a nerve. In a similar way, he flinched when I hinted at him learning from my father. In a bid to uncover what he's hiding, I again take a stab in the dark.

"Maybe it's all about pride?" I suggest, my tone neutral. "You want to follow in my father's footsteps like his perfect little progeny. But there's one problem, Colton. No matter how much you kiss his ass or do his bidding, you will *never* live up to Hale. Ever."

"Hale?" He laughs as if I compared him to a cockroach. "As if I would want to become a degenerate drug addict hellbent on destroying the only family I had. He was a liar, Frances. A pathetic, worthless piece of shit, who was more valuable dead than alive. If you ask me, I'd say what happened to him wasn't murder at all. It was a mercy killing."

"You bastard..." I swallow hard, surprised by how openly he refers to what I already know. My father intentionally killed Hale and made it look like an overdose. After leaving him to choke on his own vomit in his childhood bedroom, he paraded himself around like a martyr in hopes of being elected. With every ounce of self-control I possess, I fight back the raw, intense anger I feel. I can't play into his hands —and he *wants* me to spiral into despair.

In place of that, I propose another question. "Hale had integrity," I say, my jaw clenched. "He had a conscience, and he had a will of his own rather than be led like sheep. That's more than I can say about you. What do you think will happen when my father grows tired of you? When you've outlived your purpose? If you think owning me will earn you his loyalty, you're wrong—"

"You?" Colton snarls, lunging toward me. Both of his hands collide with my chest, shoving me against the far wall. I'm too stunned to react as he fists a hand through my hair next, wrenching my face closer to his. "You think any of this is about you? Oh, hell no, Frances. You are merely a consolation prize." He rakes his gaze up and down my body while his fingers tighten their grip until I feel the nails biting into my scalp. "A little toy they put in children's meals at fast-food restaurants. You were thrown in to merely sweeten the pot.

What your father is after, only my family can provide. He needs us far more than we need him, so keep that in mind."

Suddenly, his other hand brushes my cheek, and I wrench back. Unfazed, he lets his fingers remain in the air and flexes them so the knuckles crack in a menacing symphony. "When we are married, the things I will do to help you learn how to control that smart mouth. You'll be singing my praises like the sweet angel I know you are deep down."

"Don't touch me!" I stumble out of his reach, nearly tripping in my rush to get away. As I press my back against the wall, I have no delusions about the situation I'm in. He could do whatever he wanted to me. The fear lingers at the back of my mind, and I watch his every move while balling my hands into fists.

No. I won't let him. If he so much as twitches, I'll be ready...

But he doesn't approach. He merely tilts his head further and issues a laugh that runs through me like a knife. It's borderline gloating. Whatever truth I'd been nearing before, I've gone the wrong way.

How on earth to regroup?

I decide to play it safe for now. "I want to know when the wedding will be," I say thickly. "So that I can be prepared."

He raises an eyebrow. "You'll find out soon enough. But I can assure you that there won't be time for any games or hysterics. There is too much riding on this marriage. Should you or anyone else try to intervene, you'll face a far larger threat than I could provide."

The words hint at something. Is there another player behind the scenes in addition to my father? Someone that even Colton has the sense to fear?

He doesn't explain more before turning on his heel to leave, slamming the door in his wake.

DAZE

"LOOKS like your hunch was right on the money," Damien remarks, eyeing his cell phone. "Kane says he spotted the dad and the fiancé leaving the church. If we go now, we can tail them to the house. Maybe even figure out what they're up to. I'll drive," he says. "But you two should duck in the back. Be sure to hide those pretty fucking faces."

"Yeah, yeah, asshole."

Suddenly, he pauses, his eyes on his cell. "You aren't going to like this, Day," he says.

"What?"

"Looks like Heywood didn't want to leave your girl alone after all. He sent someone to keep an eye on her."

"Who?"

"I'll give you three guesses." Even his grimace warns that I won't like any of them, but I feel compelled to give it a try.

"I only need one," I counter. "Silas."

FREY

THERE IS TOO MUCH RIDING *on this marriage.* Colton's ominous warning echoes in my skull long after he's gone. The more time passes, the more uneasy I feel. It seems that he and my father are planning something—and I'm just a bonus prize for him and his family. Collateral.

Father wants nothing more than to be elected, but I didn't stop to think about what else he stands to gain. Or what those who support him expect.

I almost wish Colton were still here so that I could ask him what outright. Somehow, I'd make him tell me. Luckily, I have access to the next best thing. Rising to my feet, I tiptoe through the darkened space and feel for the door.

"Hello?" I call out.

Despite the fact that no one answers, I can smell a guard lurking on the other side, reeking of cigarettes and food grease. As my nostrils wrinkle, I shudder. These men don't seem to be the polished, professional bodyguards my father normally hires. They remind me more of the men I met during Daze's cage fight. Gritty. Gruff.

"I know you're there," I say, making my voice louder. "I need to use the restroom, please."

After a few seconds, the door is abruptly opened from outside.

Startled, I stumble back. My escort isn't the slender man I met earlier—someone I could try to coax into giving me information. As he towers above me, he blocks out most of the artificial light illuminating the hall. What little of him I can make out, has me swallowing hard—not a nondescript black uniform, but a T-shirt and jeans that do nothing to disguise the muscle coiled over every inch of his frame. All in all, he requires no introduction. Silas.

I spit his name out, and he laughs darkly in return.

"Your daddy wanted me to watch you personally, little girl," he explains in response to my unanswered question. His gloating expression is convincing. I almost believe him.

Almost.

"I intend to take this job seriously," he adds. "After all, there is a naughty fugitive out there, looking for you." His eyes sweep over me, raising goosebumps in their wake, but I have a hint as to why he's really here. Daze.

I take another step back, hating the weakness the action reveals. Despite his cruelty, my father isn't a fool. Leaving Silas here is the equivalent of letting a fox guard the henhouse. The criminal biker isn't in his class. Should they cross paths, I doubt he'd even acknowledge him on the street. No... Just like Silas has another aim in mind, my father wouldn't leave him to guard me without his own reasons.

Then it dawns on me—their goal is the same. Daze. What better way to lure him out of hiding than to use me? *That* is the real reason why I'm here, to act as bait.

"Ah, you don't seem very happy to see me, little girl," Silas croons. Behind him, I can see the still-open door and the darkened corridor beyond. Considering how the sound echoes, I have a horrible suspicion that he is the only one here. At least for now.

We're alone.

"Smile, little girl." His finger digs brutally into the corner of my mouth, making me grimace. I snap my teeth, barely missing his index finger. Looking at the digit in question, he laughs. "I think we're going to have a lot of fun together."

It takes me a few moments to recover from the fear, at least until I recall something Daze said to me. *Reacting out of fear is what Silas wants.*

"You can't touch me," I say, imitating his swagger.

In a rare display of shock, he cocks his head. "Is that so?" He reaches out, pressing his calloused hand against my cheek. "I think I'm touching you now."

My heart quivers. *Breathe Frey.* I can't stand how cold he is. Every cell in my body crawls with disgust. I want to run. Scream.

"You know what I mean," I reply, meeting his gaze directly. "You think that because my father lets you do his dirty work, he trusts you? No. You're merely the hired help. If you leave so much as a mark on me, he'll punish you for it." My voice sounds so confident that I almost believe it.

It's hard to tell whether Silas is fooled despite his sly grin. "I don't know if you've already forgotten, sweetheart, but I've left my mark on that pretty little face more than once." He prods the still-sore spot from when he slapped me, but I don't flinch. "Maybe I didn't make it hurt badly enough. Don't worry. We can always try again."

"That was because my father gave you your marching orders, and you carried them out like a good soldier." I feel my body go numb as his eyes flash and alarm courses through me. A heartbeat passes, but he doesn't move. Bravado or not, I wasn't too far off.

He can't touch me.

"You know it, don't you?" I choke out a hollow laugh. "You can only obey him and follow the rules he sets out. He's put you back on your leash—" My head held high, I step forward. "So, you can't touch me."

Instead of moving, he chuckles. "It seems like you learned some tricks on how to use that smart little mouth. I have to give Daze his credit. He's managed to teach you a lot in a short amount of time. Imagine what you and I will learn when we have all the time in the world to play."

My breathing hitches. "A bold claim," I manage to croak. "Seeing as how you aren't even fit enough to be by his side tonight. I'm sure Colton is," I add, thinking of what he'd hinted at earlier. "My father trusts him. Honors him. Sees him as an equal. You? You're just a useful tool."

"Is that so?" Something dark falls across his expression, and another trill of alarm runs down my spine. Then he starts to laugh, shaking his head as if in disbelief at my naivety. Instead of moving, he chuckles.

"I'm glad you find it amusing," I say. "That you know your role to play, and—"

"Listen, little girl." With one hand, he grips my throat. I feel my eyes bulge from the pressure he applies before he releases it a heartbeat later. "You think you have my balls in the palm of your hand, and that you'll be able to hide behind your daddy forever. Now, I may not know shit about politics, but most elected officials don't seem to last too long in the grand scheme of things."

I swallow hard, ignoring a twinge in my throat. Breathless, I ask, "Is that a threat?"

"No, sweetheart." He starts to stroke through my hair, and this time, I don't let myself so much as flinch. He wants to get a rise out of me. The only way to beat him is to deny him the satisfaction of knowing he's affected me. At least until he tugs, wrenching my face closer to his.

"That was a promise," he warns. "Your daddy won't be king for long, but I'll play along. Bide my time. I just hope there's something left of you when that pretty boy is finished."

His confident tone catches me off guard. It's as if he knows something I don't regarding Colton's true intentions.

A good, obedient hostage would remain silent. Luckily, more than a little of Daze's personality has rubbed off on me. It's easier now to think the way he does, and analyze things from a different perspective, even while afraid. Silas is counting on my fear to let him get away with dropping these little tidbits of information, thinking I won't notice. I need to play on that.

"As if he'd ever let you touch me," I say with every ounce of superiority I can muster. Hearing my own words echoed back to me makes me cringe. God, I sound like Colton. Or worse, my father. "Don't you get it? You're just a flunky for their benefit, but they will always regard you as trash beneath their feet."

"Is that so?" He cups my chin, wrenching my face within a mere hairsbreadth of his. I can feel his breath on my skin, hot and tinged with cigarettes. Ironically, he smells so much like Daze, but still different. What is an appealing musk on the latter, smells acrid and hostile on the man in front of me. My entire body reacts to him the same way I figure it would respond to a wild bear, or some dangerous predator. Every cell and pore is screaming at me to do only one thing.

Run.

"You've been spending too much time listening to your daddy's little sermons, sweetheart," Silas tells me. "You have a warped sense of what happens in the real world versus those scriptures he relies on so much. I'll enlighten you. He thinks he's a big shot now and that he holds all the cards. But how does that one saying go? Pride cometh before the fall?"

As he draws back, I fight to school my face into a blank expression. My mind is going a million miles a minute. He doesn't sound cocky or smug. No, he sounds convinced, as if he knows something I don't, and he's relishing in my stupidity.

"From where I'm standing, it looks like you're a good boy taking orders from someone with more power," I say.

"Oh really?" It makes my stomach churn when he laughs. "What is power but a fickle friend? It changes hands, sweetheart, sometimes more quickly than you'd think."

"Bold words." I don't miss the honesty in his voice. "What if I told my father that you were plotting behind his back?"

He smirks, amused by the threat. "Do you really think he'd believe you? After all, I'm just a dutiful little soldier. For the record, honey, I think your daddy has bigger fish to fry at the moment."

"What do you mean?"

Stepping back, he chuckles. "Wouldn't you like to know? I'm sure Daze has you convinced that I'm the bad guy. That he's as pure as driven snow and I'm a monster who only wants to see this city burn. Oh no—" He bares his teeth, his nostrils flared with anger. "I'm the only one with the balls to protect this city. It's the righteous bastards like your daddy who will gladly let the devil in. Just you wait."

He saunters into the hallway, and I follow him, unable to resist questioning. "What do you mean? You're the one who convinced my father to turn salvation into a human trafficking scheme. You're the one who wants to piggyback off his political power to hide your crimes. That doesn't sound very noble to me."

"Ah, but there is where you're wrong," he counters, shooting me a searching look from over his shoulder. "I may be the tool your daddy is using to carry out his nefarious plans, but who do you think gave him the idea in the first place? High-level trafficking doesn't seem like something you'd learn in seminary school."

"And you're just an innocent bystander waiting to take your shot at playing king?" I ask, forcing a scoff. "I may be young, but I'm not stupid, Silas."

"I'm seeing that," he says, stroking his chin once again. "No wonder you have Daze wrapped around your pretty little finger. But I'll let you in on a little secret—" His dark eyes shimmer with menace as his voice dips to a dangerously low octave. "Daze is a fucking idiot. If he were smart, he'd see the forest for the trees, but I'm betting that he's itching to play the hero. He'll come for you, and I'll gladly put a bullet in his head this time."

I can barely stomach the horrific imagery. It's not just a matter of him gloating now. He's dropping breadcrumbs to see if I'm able to pick them up. One stands out to me clearly.

"I'm a distraction," I say. While I surely realized that on my own, having him taunt me with that fact makes it clear that his feud with Daze is not his sole reason for being here. They're banking on using my captivity to draw his attention, perhaps from something else.

Whatever they're planning seems to have escaped even Colton's notice. Which means it's important. Vital. I've been focusing on the wrong piece of the puzzle all this time. Hale's death represents more than collateral damage.

"And I'm sure you know exactly who is pulling your puppet strings," I blurt out to Silas, hoping he'll be dumb enough to give me a name.

That likelihood is dashed by his smirk. "Of course, I do, baby. But do you?" He spins to face me and leans his weight against the door frame. "I'm sure you think your sordid little romance is the center of the universe, but it isn't. You're just one little buzzing fly among many. If anything, you did us a favor by keeping Daze's fucking nose out of our business for a few days."

"Oh really?" I fight to keep my face blank. "I thought he was just a fly among many."

Silas nods. "Ah, but even a fly can cause a shitload of trouble if it buzzes around the wrong person."

I hate his playful tone. He's dancing around the subject on purpose, practically goading me to ask, "Who?"

He winks. "Wouldn't you like to know? You aren't the dumb little fool I thought you were, I'll give you that. But you don't know shit, sweetheart. Not by a long shot. You're still thinking in the short-term. In small little details like you and

Daze and that little boyfriend of yours. You haven't stopped to take in the big picture. What do all those little snippets look like when viewed together?"

In other words, it's a twisted version of the puzzle analogy I used earlier. "And let me guess, you'll take pity on me and tell me your grand master plan?"

"I'll do you one better. What do they say? You give a man a fish, and he'll eat for a day, but if you *teach* a man to fish..."

He gestures for me to continue.

"He can drown you," I snap.

"No, no." He wags a finger at me disapprovingly. "You teach a man to fish, honey, and he can create a goddamn empire. Then, when you least expect it, he can take not just your fish, but your entire boat without you even realizing it. Teach a man to fish, Frey, and he can eat for life."

"And I suppose you see yourself as the winner in that scenario?"

"Better. I see myself as owning the whole damn ocean in the end. Since you seem so eager to play detective, I'll give you another tidbit. We'll make a game out of it. How about you answer a question for me? I want you to think long and hard about it. Think you can do that, honey?"

I grit my teeth, unwilling to give him a response. Even so, I can't deny that I'm intrigued. Something has him more talkative than the last time we met, and he's radiating energy like a live wire. I can either try to harness it or get shocked by it. There is no in-between.

"Fine," I hiss when he remains silent. "What is the question?"

A manic gleam ignites his expression. "I want you to riddle me this. Your mother was some rich little heiress, right?" Suddenly, anger washes over me. Blinding hot and reckless. "Don't you ever mention her—"

"She disobeyed her parents and married some poor preacher man who's lived high off her money ever since," he says over me. "I bet your daddy is terrified of that money running out, huh?" He chuckles to himself, his upper lip quirked into a sneer. "What really keeps him up at night, shaking in those polished boots? What truly feeds the ambition of a holy man?"

I can't hide my annoyance anymore. "If that's your idea of a riddle, it sucks. No wonder you resorted to a life of crime rather than poetry."

His grin doesn't even waver. "Cute. I'll rephrase—why don't you go back to the beginning, Frances?"

I hate him. Still, I'm not stupid enough to refuse to play along. If he wants to make this a game, so be it—I'm eager to know any scrap of information he'll throw my way. "The beginning," I echo. "With Hale's death?"

He chuckles, apparently enjoying this. "You've been so caught up in the saga around your dear big brother that you never stopped to think, why not you? If your daddy wanted to get him in line, why didn't he threaten *you*? I'm sure a boy scout like Hale would jump at the chance to play hero. But your daddy chose a different course of action. Why? And why hasn't he stuck a needle in your arm yet? Your brother caused him a lot less trouble, I can tell you that. Ask yourself why. And I want you to think about what other reasons that pretty boy could have for marrying you. None of them do with love, or even lust, that's for damn sure."

"What do you mean?" I hate how easily he's gotten inside my head. Already, I find myself rethinking everything I thought I knew. The scary part? He has a point—why have I been spared my father's wrath while Hale wasn't?

Even more alarming to consider, what is his real purpose for me?

"That's the point of a riddle, sweetheart," Silas explains. "Figure it out. Though, I will give you one clue to get you started. Your daddy has a trail of bodies in his wake. Start there, with his very first victim—" A sudden burst of noisy static cuts him off. I'm confused until I see him withdraw something from his pants pocket—a walkie-talkie. Holding it one-handed, he strikes a button on the end with his thumb. "What is it?"

A guttural voice comes from the other end. *"...Disturbance outside. Might be an intruder."*

A beaming smile spreads across Silas' face as he lowers the device. "Wonderful. Looks like I won our little bet. Your boyfriend is here, ready to come to the rescue. I'm more than willing to give him a nice, cozy welcome. Maybe I'll even let you watch."

"Wait!" Despite knowing I cannot physically stop him, I step forward. God, I hope they're wrong. *Please, Daze...* I pray that he didn't come. "What did you mean about my father?"

He winks. "We can chat more later. In fact, tonight, I'm going to be your special friend. We'll be arm-in-arm when Daze comes. In the meantime, how about I tell you a story? The story of the first woman Daze Keaton fucked over and destroyed."

Jaw clenched, I brace myself for what he might say next—this isn't the first time he's brought up this certain topic. Daze was once in love with a woman named Renna—Silas' sister.

"I don't think you're ready yet," he croons, his breath hot on my face. "But soon, little girl. I'll teach you how a real man is supposed to be."

"Like you?" I scoff. "In that case, I'd choose a so-called piece of shit like Daze any day."

He grunts, but doesn't react with the violence I expect. His touch is gentle as he bats a piece of stray hair from my face.

"Oh, sweetheart. One day, you're going to eat those words, and I'll be waiting."

He turns and enters the hall, slamming the door behind him.

And if Daze is really somewhere on the property, I pray that he stays out of sight.

FIVE

DAZE

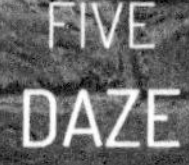

"BEN, tell me again how being here is smart and not a fucking waste of time," I mutter under my breath to the man crouched beside me behind an overgrown hedge bush. There's a plastic gnome nearby, bathed in the orange glow of sunset. Its goofy grin seems mocking. I bet that happy bastard thinks I'm an idiot.

So do I.

"You're being smart," Ben counters while juggling a pair of binoculars with one hand. "Or at least, I thought so before we were kneeling in fucking dirt for two goddamn hours. Now I think you may or may not be a dumbass. The jury's still out."

"Fuck," I hiss, though my voice doesn't rise above a whisper. "Frey's stuck with those monsters, enduring God knows what, and we're here. Watching her daddy play fucking tea party. Unless his wife is secretly a cartel goon, I doubt she's the one he answers to."

"That's a negative," Marco replies without missing a beat. He's positioned further back, serving as a lookout. So far, he's been quiet and unobtrusive, but I can see his gaze even in the dark. He's watching things closely, missing nothing.

This empty house near the Heywood mansion provides a good vantage point to observe them, but it's still a distance away. From here, we only have a view of the west end of the house, and precisely one dining room window. Even so, being that it's out of range from the guards milling around the property, this place makes for the perfect staging area for what should have been a tense fucking stakeout that would lead to answers and make Frey proud.

Instead, we're already past the main course, and only Heywood and his wife are seated at the table. Judging from the stiff but steady way they eat, I doubt they're expecting any guests. Still, I have a whole new appreciation for Frey, just getting a glimpse of the environment she had to tolerate.

Her father is a bastard. Watching the prick incites a rage that I haven't felt since he tried to put me in prison. Even from here, I can sense his cold hatred. The poor woman beside him is cowering in his wake. When I think of Frey in close proximity to this man, my blood boils.

But I can't do a damn thing about any of it.

"That's it. I'm going to the church." I start to inch back. "Fuck this. I can meet up there with Kane. Frey needs me more than this bullshit—"

"Wait." Ben reaches out for my arm, but I shake him off.

"No. Enough playing babysitter—"

"Will you just wait? Look!"

I turn back to the house and find Heywood and his wife still seated at the dining table. "What? Just admit it, Ben. You like being a fucking voyeur—"

"Look at the road," Marco pitches in. He's drawn closer, his eyes fixed straight ahead. "There."

He's pointing to the lifeline running through the heart of this gated community, where headlights pierce the darkness. Instantly, I shut my mouth. "Son of a bitch." I drop down next to Ben, knocking over our gnome sidekick in the process.

Someone's arriving, alright. From here, I can't be completely sure, but they don't seem to be Silas. In fact, the figure surrounded by police cars is the last person I'd suspect would be meeting with Heywood.

"That's the police commissioner," Marco remarks, crouching beside me. "I know that face. He did all kinds of dealings with Cortez. Usually making sure the police stayed out of his way."

"Doesn't look like he's on duty, that's for damn sure," Ben remarks beside me. "What could he want with Heywood?"

"Don't know," I hiss. "Doesn't look like he's here to bust the bastard for kidnapping either. I wish we could hear what they're saying."

"Speak of the fucking devil, and he shall appear." A figure dressed in all black vaults over the hedge bush just feet away. I tense, readying for a fight. Then I recognize the figure's crazy-ass grin and gleaming green eyes. "Did you miss me?" Damien pulls himself upright and withdraws something from his pocket. "You can thank Lex for this. He planted a bug on the outside of the window before we arrived. He said he nearly got his head blown off in the process, so this better be worth it."

"Did you check out how many guards he has on him?"

"Too many to take on with the four of us," he replies with a shrug. Then, he extends the tiny device on the palm of his hand. "Now shut the fuck up, and let's see what the bastard is really up to."

"How do you work this thing?" Marco wonders.

"Well, turn it on for starters," Damien explains. "Now you just twist that little dial until—yeah, we should hear something through it now. Just wait."

Amid a rustling of static, I can barely make out the tinkling of silverware. Heywood and his wife have finished eating, and she's gathering the dishes at full speed. Their apparent guest hasn't even entered the house and it's like the entire mood has changed. The wife is edgy, practically racing around the room to clear the table amid the thud of what must be plates. Heywood, however, remains seated, watching her work. They don't trade a single word, making it hard to know if the bug is working or not. At least until a new figure says, "The commissioner has arrived, sir."

"Good." Finally, Heywood rises to his feet and moves out of range of the window. "Show him in."

Heywood's wife keeps fiddling with something at her place setting, picking it up. Setting it down. Finally, she sighs.

"Michael, I know you're upset with Frances, but do you really think she should stay there all night? Would it be so bad to let her stay in her old room? I could watch her—"

"Enough," Heywood snaps, rendering her silent. "Don't make a scene before our guests."

As he speaks, more people enter the room, but I can only make out shuffling sounds and terse greetings. The guest of honor chooses to sit just out of view of the window, preventing a clear shot with either the binoculars or a camera.

"Smart fucker," I mutter under my breath. "This isn't their first rodeo."

"No, it isn't," Marco agrees. "This whole setup has the air of a high-stakes meeting. Done out in the open but with coded words and shit, so nothing can be proven. Yeah, the cops can say that you two met, but they can't confirm that anything was discussed other than wedding plans and kids. They just didn't realize that 'plans' was code for gun smuggling."

"I'm sure my old man used that trick once or twice in his day," I say coldly. "I wonder what code words Heywood uses."

"Well, let's hope we can find out," Ben says. Suddenly he cocks his head and gestures to the bug.

"Good evening," Heywood says, "I'm surprised you could stop by on such short notice."

I instantly react to the ice in his tone. This isn't a happy little meeting, it seems. No. The tension is so thick I could slice it with one of those fancy butter knives.

"Yes, well, I've been keeping abreast of your election, and I wanted to touch base with the man at the center of such chaos. You've been a busy man, Heywood."

"That doesn't sound very friendly," Ben whispers.

I nod, still listening.

Despite the obvious hostility, the next few minutes pass in relative polite monotony. Boring, basic bullshit that could be the poorly-written script of some shitty sitcom rather than anything a normal couple would talk about.

Again, this whole mess is starting to feel like a waste of time.

"Daze!" Ben rams my shoulder, snapping me out of the murderous fantasy. "You hear that?"

"What?" I focus back on the receiver. Heywood and his visitor are still talking, but the mood has decidedly changed.

"...arrangements have been made, I hope."

"Yes," Heywood replies. "When I am elected, we can commence with the plan immediately."

"Good," the visitor replies. "With emergency powers, we can cleanse this city with hellfire and start anew."

"There is one problem," Heywood adds. "My daughter. She's proven difficult—"

"Ah, but you need her to provide the proper collateral," the man replies. "Without that money, our agreement can't be fulfilled, I'm afraid. You'll have to find another disaster to take advantage of."

Another disaster? I look at Ben and see him frown, picking up on the phrasing as well.

"I don't expect this to delay anything," Heywood clarifies. "I merely meant to inform you that there will be an accelerated timeline. The wedding will happen sooner than expected."

"Oh?"

"Tomorrow night," Heywood replies. "I hope you will attend."

"Don't," Ben hisses, placing a hand on my shoulder.

Belatedly, I realize that he did it to keep me from lurching to my feet. Somehow, I keep my head down.

"Of course," the man replies. "I wouldn't miss it. The dawn of a new era is one that cannot be overlooked. I see it as a good omen for what we have planned for the city as a whole. I'm looking forward to it."

They trade more dry-as-hell conversation, and then the visitor leaves.

"Well, that was interesting," Marco says. "Looks like their code words are a bit more vague than ours."

"Fuck that. You heard what the bastard said. You're crazy if you think I'm going to sit here and let that wedding happen."

"I don't expect you to, Day. But I do want you to think. Think things through. They're counting on you making an ass of yourself by jumping the gun. You proved them wrong tonight. That was good. You need to keep your head high. Don't get distracted now. Let's come up with a plan."

"Fine." He's right, as much as it stings to admit. "But if you think I'm going to sit by and let Frey marry that bastard, you have another thing coming."

"Oh, I don't think you should sit by at all," Damien says with a dangerous laugh. He licks his lips, eyeing the Heywood mansion. "In fact, I think we should get a few suits and shit ready. It looks like we have a fancy shindig to crash."

"Hell yes," I say in a rush. "I couldn't agree more."

SIX

FREY

IT'S STRANGE WATCHING SILAS' cocky demeanor wear away as the hours tick by without Daze's arrival. It happens in stages, first with increasing agitation. Eventually, a fidgety, restlessness has him pacing my narrow cell as I watch. As night fades into dawn, rage consumes him.

All without so much as a knock on the door from a certain blond outlaw.

"I guess your hero decided you weren't worth it at all," Silas snaps to me as he finally heads for the door.

I can't deny that the insinuation stings, though for very different reasons than I think he suspects. I'm so damn worried about him and Sammy. What if this was all a sick display for my benefit, and they're both dead, rotting in my father's basement. That's the real reason he's kept me here all night.

To torture them.

To torture me.

Even before the thought fully finishes forming, I bat it aside. If my father had Daze in his grasp, he'd want me to hear—or better yet, witness—him being tormented and punished.

That prospect gives me a small, twisted bit of comfort. At least I have hope that he's okay.

Though that says little for me. As Silas storms to the room, he turns to face me one last time. "Remember what I've told you, sweetheart," he snarls. "Remember the kind of monster that you've chosen to let into your bed. Sooner or later, Daze will get bored of you. Though hell, it looks like he already has. Just in the nick of time, too. From what I hear, you're going to be a busy girl for the next few days."

I shiver at the malice in his tone. "What do you mean?"

"I'll let you stew on it." He laughs, his eyes glittering. "Bye, bye for now, sweetheart."

When the door slams in his wake, I sink to the floor, exhausted. I never realized how much strength it takes to remain strong and unaffected by an enemy in your midst. As much as I hate to admit it, I can't get his words out of my head.

Renna, his sister, was with Daze, and she died of an overdose that Silas seems to think was intentional. The similarities to Hale's death are too close for comfort. Almost as if the killer were mocking him with the method.

But why?

The mystery swirls in my mind, and I'm distracted by my surroundings. I hope Daze followed up with the reporter. Maybe he's found an answer to the many loose ends and missing threads that Hale left behind. I feel like I'm drowning in all the deception and lies, unable to find a sturdy lifeline to pull myself out of the mire.

In the end, I wind up replaying my last few moments with Daze over and over in my mind. I miss him in a way I don't expect. It's a physical ache that goes deeper than any pain I've ever felt, stealing my breath away whenever I try to decipher it. I miss his voice and the warmth of his arms around me. I crave the safety of lying beside him, feeling his heartbeat thump beneath his skin.

I miss being someone other than good, innocent, weak Frey. With Daze, I felt...powerful. A force to be reckoned with, unwilling to take shit from anyone. Deep down, I still *am* that woman.

Then and there, crouched on the floor, I come up with a plan that feels so reckless my heart skips a beat at the thought of carrying it out. Good girls don't contemplate the very, very bad things I am considering.

Maybe that's a good thing.

Being an angel is overrated. Maybe I always was a devil at heart.

It feels like another hour passes before a familiar guard appears at my door to escort me to the bathroom. I tidy up and wash my hair several times in the sink with just water and hand soap, eager to erase Silas' musk from my skin. On the way back to my cell, my eyes are drawn to a set of glass doors near the entrance that let in a stream of pale light.

"Is my father coming today?" I ask the guard. "Or Colton?"

In response, he grunts a noncommittal sound and curtly ushers me back inside my cell. My question is answered soon after anyway by twin footsteps marching in my direction. One set is familiar, carrying the smug air of Colton. The other, I recognize as well, and my stomach churns in grim acknowledgment. My father.

Both take their time approaching my door and then wait as a few excruciating seconds pass before the door opens.

"Frances," my father says. "I hope you've had time to think about your actions."

I audibly gasp as I take him in. His blue eyes stand out even more starkly in contrast to his black suit and navy tie. To maintain his obsession with neatness, his hair is slicked back, exposing the hollow panes of his face. It's the same impeccable image he's always projected—minus one little flaw. It's so obscure that I don't think anyone else would even notice, but I've learned to recognize my father's various moods over the years.

Especially when he's furious.

As old childish fear flutters through my chest, I can't resist taking a step back. His worst moments come when he is like this—both cruel and suave, coaxing his victim into submission. It's strange how I never classified it as what it was before. I would attribute his mood swings to stress or pressure. The truth is, at his core, he has always been the same person.

An angry, violent man who has little self-control.

"I was fine," I say. "In fact, I rather enjoyed having someone keep me company."

He raises an eyebrow, but Colton speaks first.

"Company? Who do you mean?"

"The man from the gang," I say, being deliberately vague. "He stayed with me all night, waiting just outside my door. How kind of you to ask him to look over me."

They both trade looks—obviously, Silas' stunt wasn't planned. Knowing that doesn't comfort me any, quite the opposite. He's becoming reckless, emboldened enough to eschew my father's rules and boundaries. Why?

"Uncultured swine," Colton snarls under his breath. "I hope you didn't show him the same hospitality you show to other men of his ilk."

I smile as though his disdain were a badge of honor. "I guess you'll have to ask him. Though I wouldn't mind if he returned when you leave. He told me some rather interesting stories."

My father's eyes narrow. I'm treading on dangerous ground. Goading him into a rage now would provide a petty bit of satisfaction, but it's far better to wait and see how Silas' obvious defiance lands on its own.

So, I bite my tongue.

Colton looks back warily at his elder. As he returns his gaze to me, I notice a change in him that I didn't see yesterday. He'd been angry then but restrained, as if biding his time. In the present... His energy is boundless and unsteady. He reminds me of a kid with a secret, bursting at the seams with excitement. Apprehension tightens my throat. Whatever could make him so antsy doesn't bode well for me.

Not in the slightest.

"I thought it would be prudent to inform you myself," my father says. "So that you can prepare yourself mentally."

Trying to keep my voice steady, I take a deep breath. "Prepare myself for what?"

"For your marriage," Father replies. "I've decided that you will marry Colton tonight."

A crushing disappointment washes over me, and it's all I can do to remain standing. I knew this was coming, and I knew that I would have to face this challenge alone.

That doesn't make it any easier to keep my head held high, knowing what they have in store for me. They want to see me cower and plead. I refuse to give them the satisfaction.

"Where?" I ask dryly. "I would think you would want it to be here in the church."

His smile widens, and I feel a genuine stab of fear and panic. My father may have intimidated me my entire life, but I've never felt this darkness in him before. Not even when he whipped me. His ultimate aim is far more sinister than trying to control me.

What is it? I have no idea.

"It will be in a house of God," he says cryptically. "Which is far more than you deserve."

A house of God. I ruminate over those words, seeking out the obvious clue hidden within them. His cold gaze suggests he doesn't expect this to be the grand social event he had envisioned just a few weeks ago.

It's more like an execution, if not of my life, then my very freedom.

"Where," I repeat.

His head inclined toward Colton, he ignores me. "Leave us."

"But sir, I—"

"Now."

Colton retreats down the hall with one last frustrated glance at me while Father remains at the doorway. For a long few seconds, he just stares at me as if he's trying to reconcile the figure he sees with the little girl who used to follow in his wake, hanging on his every word.

The memories hurt to relive. We were so happy together, the three of us. I hadn't even picked up any change in him when he married Catherine. While running the church and his political campaigns, I wrote up his increasing sternness as misplaced stress. Now, however, it's easier to pinpoint the various moments where his true colors began to emerge, long before these last few years. Among all the signs, the clearest stands out like a neon sign.

The day of my mother's funeral.

"It hurts me to see you like this, Frances," he says, scanning my rumpled clothing and disheveled hair. In his eyes, I see emptiness, not pain. He lingers on my bruised, swollen face, and I swear the corner of his upper lip twitches into the shadow of a grin. "So lost amid your own sinful ways," he continues. "Unable to see the righteous path shining before you. A lesser father would have already turned his back on you, but I refuse to do so."

"A lesser father," I repeat hoarsely. "A *good person* would have never resorted to kidnapping and threatening a little boy just to get his way. He wouldn't have killed his own son, and he certainly wouldn't have murdered his first wife."

I don't know how I expect those jabs to land, but I figure that nothing I'd imagine could ever come close to the reality. In the face of the truth, he never recoils. He doesn't even glower in anger. His only response is to stare, as if he has become so numb to violence that he isn't even aware of its horror.

It's a detached apathy I never even saw in Daze—as if he has lost all humanity.

"You are so misguided, my dear child," I hear him say as he strokes my hair without warning. His fingers tug and snag on loose stands, pulling at my scalp. Suddenly, he captures my chin in a rigid grip and angles my face so that our gazes meet. A cold stare greets me in return. "So long in the darkness that you can't find your way back with prayer alone. No more will I ignore your plight. Just as I intend to save this entire city, I will make it my mission to save you as well."

His tone makes me shiver. He seems to be referring to a lot more than just marriage. Something more twisted than that, but I can't even open my mouth to ask what it is. I'm paralyzed.

"After tonight, you will fulfill your final duty to me. Then, I will fulfill my obligation to you. I see the truth now. What you really need."

An icy, creeping sensation washes over me, starting at my head and crawling downward. With it comes a wave of nausea and a sick sense of foreboding that urges me to run. Now. If I don't, I may never get the chance to do so again.

Instead, I hold his gaze and croak, "What is that?"

"Salvation," he says. "After some reflection, I realized that there was only one clear path. You think I failed your mother, but that is where you are wrong. She failed you. It was my duty to make you see that, and I failed. It's only logical that you would follow in her path, devoid of proper guidance. I should have seen then what I do now. There is only one way to break the cycle and salvage this family line. One way to save your soul, and I refuse to lose you to the devil."

"Like you lost Hale?" I ask.

"Hale? He was a test of my faith, much like the one God himself presented to Abraham, but you... You are a mission. One I have gravely neglected. The path to hell began with a mere apple from a poisoned tree. To prevent such an insidious force from taking over his garden, it wasn't enough for Adam to merely prevent Eve from eating the forbidden fruit. By then, it was already too late. He needed to chop down the tree at its root and stop Eve's corruption before it was too late. For you, it is not too late, Frances."

"What do you mean?"

"I'm willing to do for you what I couldn't do for your brother, or even your mother. I'm going to save your soul."

The unsettling feeling in my stomach grows stronger as he pulls back. His words conceal a hidden threat, but I can't discern what it is. The word "salvation" means something very different to him today than it does in the Bible.

Don't get distracted, Frey, a part of me warns. *You're here for a reason. Take advantage of this moment.*

"I know about the construction company," I say, desperate to regain some semblance of even footing. "The one Colton's family owns. I know that you need it to help carry out whatever nefarious plans you have in mind for Salvation. Is that why you want me to marry him so badly that you'll do it in the dead of night like some kind of human trafficker?"

His eyes narrow, and a flush creeps over his cheeks. Without really even trying to get under his skin, I've done that and more. Somewhere within that rant was a barb that hit the sweet spot.

"I knew it was a mistake to let your brother remain in our lives after he chose to corrupt his body with poison," Father says. His voice rises in pitch, rippling with barely-concealed anger. "I spared you the reality of that, and let you turn your helpless anger to me. A good father knows when to yield to the needs of his flock. I gave you that small bit of grace." He reaches out, brushing the tip of a long finger against my cheek. "But no more."

I don't even see the slap coming. Just the stars that spot my vision next. The world bucks beneath me, and the next thing I know, I'm crouched on the floor, cradling my throbbing cheek against my palm. Tears spring from my eyes, but I grit my teeth rather than let them fall. I can't allow the display of violence to deter me. If Daze were here, I know what he'd say —*You're on track. You've got him cornered.*

"Hale was never the sick one, was he?" I croak. My mouth fills with a bitter taste, and I shudder once I realize what it is —blood. I have to choke down a swallow just to keep talking. At the same time, I lurch to my feet, forced to sway unsteadily. "He wasn't the one who betrayed our family in the blind pursuit of greed, was he? It was always you, willing to harm anyone who got in your way. Hale wasn't the only one, either. I'm sure my mother saw through you on day—"

Another blow strikes the unguarded side of my face, and I hit the floor on my hands and knees. My eyes are streaming, my jaw on fire. I suck in air through my nose as more blood dribbles down my chin. *Breathe, Frey. Focus!*

"Your mother was my very first mistake," Father says, his voice sounding disjointed as if coming from several directions at once. "My first bite of the poisoned apple. I thought I could change her heathen ways and mold her into the woman she was destined to be. I see now that I was wrong. She was already beyond saving—"

Wham! A sharp pressure rams into my side, knocking the air from my lungs. Gasping, I wheeze, curled in a ball as my father's booted foot comes to rest inches from my head.

"As dark as your path may seem, there is still hope for you, Frances. I know that. I can feel it, and I refuse to fail you again."

"If murder is your idea of saving, then I think I'll be better off in hell," I spit.

He steps closer, and my body instinctively tenses up for another blow, but one doesn't come. Instead, he tilts his head to observe me as if for the first time. I don't like the look in his eye. It's too sharp, lingering over my trembling legs in a way that raises goosebumps all over my skin. It's the same way Silas looked at me, but different. Darker. Twisted.

"You think your mother was some paragon of virtue?" he hisses. "The bitch who schemed and lied to put you in her rightful place? Oh, I'm sure she never told you that, did she."

"What are you talking about?"

"I didn't find out until she was already long gone, the sick little game she played. Changing her will at the last damn minute. Only one obstacle remains in my way now... Innocent Frances, whom her very spirit has corrupted to follow in her footsteps. My daughter is gone, isn't she? It's you in her place, isn't it, laughing at me from beyond the grave." He seizes a fistful of my hair and wrenches me to my feet.

"It's you," he breathes out, his wide eyes on my face. His jaw is slack, his skin pale. It's like he's seeing a ghost in my place. "It was always you, possessing her. Turning her away from me just as you did my only son. Hale was your first victim, wasn't he? It was you that corrupted his mind, goading him to stick his nose where it didn't belong. You think you can win, demon? I won't let your evil taint the world any longer."

"Who?" I rasp. "Who do you think I am? Look at me!"

It's like he doesn't even hear me, but when a single name leaves his lips, I have my answer. "Abagail," he says hoarsely. "It's you, isn't it? Laughing from your damned grave. I won't let you have her. I'll drive you out myself if I have to. I already defeated you once—I'll do it again."

My mind is left reeling. *Abagail?* Has he finally lost his hold on reality?

His hands go for my neck, grasping, squeezing. I can't resist my instinct to fight back, kicking, scraping at his fingers, clawing at his forearms. It's no use, and a cold sense of finality washes over me as, bit by bit, the strength starts to leave my limbs. This is how I die.

At the hands of my own father...

"Sir?" The other voice comes from down the hall, drawing my father's attention. Suddenly, he releases me, and I gulp for breath.

"What is it?" Father demands, turning to the figure approaching him.

"We should leave now. If you want to make it in time, sir."

Make it? To where?

"Yes, of course." Clearing his throat, my father adjusts his askew collar, his composed self once more. Whatever this is about must be important. Important enough for him to casually swipe my blood off his knuckles and turn to leave.

"Tonight, Abagail," he calls back to me. "Once your plans are circumvented, I'll send you back to hell."

As he leaves, my mind reels. It's the second time he's called me by my mother's name, a coincidence I'd be a fool to overlook. There's something important in that slipup, and I doubt that Colton's wedding plans are at the forefront of my father's mind. He's planning something else, and I need to warn Daze. But how?

"It hurts me to see you like this, do you realize that?" The voice is Colton's. I didn't even see him come in, but he's kneeling beside me, dabbing at my face with a handkerchief.

I cringe out of his reach, biting back the pain. "Don't touch me."

He sighs. "Frances. I will admit that I find your newfound rebellious streak enticing, but remember that I will have years to break you after our wedding. From the moment I first saw you, I knew you were destined to be mine. From the start. I've bided my tongue and been patient, but now..." He sneers, and for a split second, I don't even recognize him. "Now I see that the only way to make you mine, is by demanding it. No matter what you or your father or anyone else thinks!"

"Will you?" I counter. Somehow, I manage to keep my voice flat and neutral. Inside, I'm shaking. This man before me is a stranger, capable of anything. Even so, provoking him is my best shot at gaining the upper hand. "My father didn't seem to think so," I add to twist the knife.

Predictably, Colton's eyes narrow, and he draws back, wringing the bloodied kerchief between his fingers. "You were always a righteous little bitch," he snarls. "But you were never one for riddles. What exactly are you implying?"

"Nothing," I say, thinking quickly. "I just wonder if you realize who is really in control. It isn't you."

He scoffs. "Frances, petty, childish, mind games are beneath you. Besides, should your father want to 'be in control,' as you put it, he would still need me." He smirks, his eyes gleaming with a smugness that makes my skin crawl.

"How so?"

He looks me up and down, deliberately pausing over my breasts. When I cross my arms over my chest, he finally meets my gaze. "Because the only way to fulfill the terms of your inheritance requires that you either reach the age of twenty-five, or are legally married first. In case of the second scenario, you'd only get fifty percent, unless, of course..." He leans in to mockingly whisper, "You have a child soon after. Your father needs your husband if he wants to fulfill the terms of the contract."

"What contract? What the hell are you talking about?" I demand.

"Your mother's will," he says. "Hale would have been eligible for his share, but your father took care of that, didn't he? With the eldest of her two children dead, the full bulk of her inheritance goes to you. I'm sure you realized that. It's why you've been poking your nose where it doesn't belong, pretending that you were doing it out of righteous love. I'm sure the truth is that you just wanted to make sure that his death wouldn't affect your half of the fortune."

"What fortune?"

He raises an eyebrow. "I've found the feisty version of you tiresome, but I will admit that I prefer it to the innocent little Frances who always looks at the world with that wide-eyed naivety. You know damn well what I'm talking about."

I can sense his irritation. If I want him to keep talking, I need to tread carefully. So, I face him and let myself visibly wince.

"I'm sorry. You're right. I do know, but my question is, how do you plan to circumvent that. Once I'm married, there is no use for you anymore, is there?"

He frowns. "Don't play coy, or did you not hear the second part of the stipulation? Your father already gets half of the money once you say, 'I do.' Unless he plans to keep you around for another two years, then you need an heir sooner rather than later if you're to receive the full inheritance. Nine months may seem like a long time, but I'm sure seven or eight will do. Then, if anything happens to either of you, the money goes to your husband. Your father has no ties in any case. Your mother made sure of that."

My mother, the woman I spent so much of my life believing had abandoned me. What if that, among almost everything else, had also been a lie? She hasn't been living out on her own all this time, and what if her addiction hadn't been her own choice? What if, just like Hale, her supposed downfall had been entirely manufactured for one purpose only?

I lick my lips, still tasting blood. My bottom one must be split, and it stings like hell. It's getting harder to keep my left eye open. The pain hasn't sunk in yet, but I'm well aware of the fact that time is running out. Somehow, I need to free myself and warn Daze. There isn't even time to agonize over a course of action. I just need to do something.

"You're right," I say thickly. "No matter what, he'll need you. But I don't think he's in his right mind anymore, Colton. Have you stopped to think about that?"

He laughs. "Do you really think I'm that much of a fool? That you can just bat your eyes at me, and I'll come running. You aren't that good of an actress, Frances. Besides, I saw the way you looked at him, that cretin."

My entire body reacts to the mere hint of Daze. I can't help it. I know the longing for him shows on my face, and I can't even begin to hide it. Instead, I meet Colton's gaze directly and try to hunt for some small shred of emotion I can use to my benefit. Beneath the hate and anger, I find a glimpse of something useful.

Lust.

"You don't want to hurt me," I tell him. "You don't."

"I would beg to differ, Frances." He reaches out to stroke my hair, only to grab a handful of strands and yank. "After the humiliation you've put me through, before your father. Before the entire congregation. Do you have any idea what you've done? My own father can barely look at me, and yet here I still am, sacrificing my integrity to save your honor. I think that's earned me a bit of a reward, wouldn't you say?"

He presses his mouth cruelly to mine in a painful, sloppy imitation of a kiss.

I can't silence a cry, but I don't pull away. Eyes streaming, I meet his gaze directly until he's the one forced to look away first. As he releases me, I bite on my swollen lip just to keep from whimpering. It hurts. Every part of me is on fire, and I know at the back of my mind that I won't be able to handle this kind of treatment for very long. Sooner or later, I'm going to break.

I hear a voice in my head that sounds suspiciously like Daze say, *Do something about it. Fight. You don't want me to save you, princess? Then you better fucking get a move on saving yourself.*

"You want me," I say, changing tact. "I know you do, and I still want you too. You can't blame me for trusting the first person to give me answers, can you? You know how worried I was about Hale. You know that all I wanted was to find out why."

"And have you?" He's smug again, his smile a sneer. "I don't think you have, Frances. Because there is one part of your role to play that I don't think even your father has told you yet."

"And what is that?"

He rises to his feet. "Play your cards right and be the obedient fiancée until tonight. Then, after our wedding, I'll enlighten you. Perhaps I might even take pity on you enough to help change your father's mind. But know this. When you are my wife, his rules will no longer apply to you. You will answer only to me, and I won't tolerate a deceitful woman in my home. You will learn to be subservient, even if I have to beat the goodness into you."

"Tonight, then," I say, watching him leave. The second he slams the door behind him, I don't waste any time. I slide his cell phone from its hiding place between my legs and fumble to get it open. It's locked, but I get it open on my first try— our supposed anniversary. The thought makes me sick as I open up a message and compile one on the fly. Then I send it to a number I've memorized by heart. My fingers tremble as I hit send at the same time I hear footsteps rushing toward the door. I delete the message and slide the phone away just in time to witness Colton fling it open, his cheeks pink, chest heaving.

"What's wrong?" I ask with faked innocence. Sweat is dripping down my neck, and I just hope he underestimates me enough to write off the reaction as fear.

As he surveys me, his eyes narrow before he turns his attention to the floor. As soon as he spots the phone near the doorway, he crouches to pick it up, holding it as warily as he would a live viper. I can't tell what he thinks as he tucks it in his pocket. Does he know I used it? Will he somehow be able to track the number down?

Hopefully, Daze won't try to call back.

Without a word, Colton turns on his heel and storms off, and I can finally breathe again. Then, I clear my mind of fear and focus on another plan for escape. One that utilizes the razor blade tucked into my hem.

Do I have what it takes to use it?

It only takes thinking about Daze in danger and his beautiful eyes swollen with pain for me to find the answer. Hell yes. I'll find my way back to him no matter what it takes.

Or who I have to kill in the process.

SEVEN

DAZE

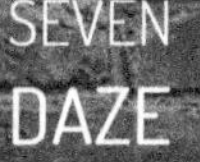

LOVE CAN UTTERLY FUCK you up. You think you're on the right path, and you know what's best. Then, before you know it, you're pussy-whipped, shackled by someone else's morals and ideals. You can't react out of anger and impulse like you used to. You can't barge in to save them either, spraying bullets and dropping bodies. You'd rather die than have them hate you.

Or worse.

Fear you.

So, to prove your worth to them, you strangle your worst impulses. As soon as I saw Sam for the first time, I knew I would die for him. In Frey's case, however, there is no parental bond to hide behind. The sex alone doesn't seem to justify this change that I can feel warping me from within. No, it's like she's altering me on a cellular fucking level, and the worst part?

I *like* it, to some extent, the shit she does to me. Fuck, she's more potent than a drug, making me feel like more than a worthless piece of shit. She makes me feel alive again. Powerful.

And she makes me terrified to lose that high.

"You seem tense," Ben says. The irony is he's the one hunched over a table scattered with journal pages, trying to make sense of Hale's lost, rambling words. "Shouldn't you be relieved? You heard from her. You know she's still alive and able to type, at least. Shouldn't that be a good thing?"

It is.

But then it isn't.

If she's taken the risk to steal a phone, then she's desperate. I'd be a fool to just twiddle my fucking thumbs out here, following the breadcrumbs she's dropped.

Deep down, though... I suspect that's exactly what she wants me to do. Trust her. Lay the groundwork to make sure her father can't fuck with her or anyone else ever again.

So, I'll play. I'll be fucking Hansel and Gretel and keep unraveling the mystery of Michael Heywood and whatever the fuck he's up to.

"She said that something's happening tonight," I say to Ben, who's still watching me. "We should keep an eye on Heywood."

"I bet it has something to do with the meeting last night," Ben agrees.

"But that isn't all. Something's off. I can feel it. She's keeping something back from me. I know her."

"Do you really?" Ben counters. At the look I shoot him, he immediately throws his hands into the air. "Look, all I'm saying is that, what? You've only known her for two weeks. I get the whole Romeo and Juliet thing is sexy, but let's not go overboard."

"That's not what I mean," I snap. "There's more to it. I can tell when she's afraid, even without seeing her face. Something is wrong. I'm just not sure what."

"You know the drill," Ben says. "We keep an eye on Silas and Heywood. We continue to build the crew. Then you get to be the hero and rescue your damsel in distress."

"Were you able to track down that reporter?" I ask a figure lurking at the back of the room. Skinny, with a mop of black hair, he looks at home seated before a mess of computer equipment that seemingly appeared overnight. I can't imagine him holding his own in an arena, but I've heard the rumors. His speed and size are two weapons he's adept at using to his advantage.

"Almost," Lex replies. "He's a squirely one, and he knows how to cover his tracks. The bastard's been posting status updates to social media but using an IP spoofer to disguise his—"

"I think I can follow, but you might want to dumb it down for the others," I interject.

"Yeah." The man laughs. "It means that he's a tricky fucker to pin down. He has a listed address registered with the paper, but I doubt he'd be lying low there. No, if it were me, I'd be hiding in plain sight. The only way to hook someone like this is to draw them out. We need bait."

"Why can't we just say that we got his name from Frey?" I suggest.

"A guy this wound up? He probably won't believe it," Lex counters. "We gotta lure him to a meeting—and it's gotta be juicier than a simple meet and greet. Something he'd risk his life over."

"What about knowing what went down during Heywood's little get-together last night?"

He winks. "That'll do it. But how to set the bait? If we're hunting him down, you can bet that Silas and Heywood have already caught on. They could be trolling the same fucking database, ready to ambush any meeting we might set up. Plus, this dude is far too paranoid to take a risk without knowing there'll be a payoff. We'll get one shot at messaging him, and we gotta make it count."

"Fuck that. I don't do cloak-and-dagger shit. We lay it on the table, and maybe we can kill two birds with one stone."

"So what do we do?"

"We send them a fucking picture."

He raises his eyebrows. "That's not exactly subtle."

"We send a message. One so juicy that the reporter won't be able to resist, and if Heywood and his goons are watching, they won't be able to ignore it, either. All we have to do is wait and see who comes to nibble."

"I wouldn't exactly call that a smart plan," Lex says. "But it's crazy enough to work, if only to get us all killed. Count me in."

"And what should we do in the meantime?" Ben asks. "Just in case we all don't die, and this turns out to give us the leverage we need."

"Well then..." I shrug, thinking it over. "Then times up, and if Frey isn't free by then, we'll blow that fucking church to hell and back. I don't give a damn."

"That's the Day I know," Ben says, chuckling. "I thought I'd lost you there for a moment. But there is one more thing we need to worry about," he adds. "Something that, if you don't take care of it now, might kill you before Silas or anyone else gets the chance."

"And what is that?"

He shrugs and raises an eyebrow as if to say, what do you think? "Your sister."

She's lived in the same house for the past ten years, and it's fucking easy to break into. All you have to do is find the spare key under the mat in the backyard and unlock the door.

Usually, I could sneak in through the kitchen and help myself to whatever leftovers she had in the fridge before she ever noticed I was there.

Today seems no different. The place is unguarded, and when I enter the kitchen, I'm tense at the silence I hear inside. The TV isn't on, and I don't hear Sam's usual chatter. Then I feel the pressure against the back of my neck, and I realize the awful truth.

I've fucked up.

"I'm going to warn you bastards one more time," Lyra snarls. "I don't know where the fuck Daze is, and if Silas wants to look for him, he's more than welcome to come pull up a fucking chair, but the next time he sends some fucking stranger into my house, I won't be so nice—"

"Thank fuck," I say, holding my hands up in surrender. "You aren't entirely goddamn stupid. You kept the gun."

She scoffs and pulls back. I turn to see her holding a shotgun —one that I bought for her years ago and one she'd sworn she'd gotten rid of. It looks well maintained, and I can tell it's loaded. Good.

"Daze? Have you lost your fucking mind? Do you have any idea how worried I've been?"

"Yeah, yeah. I know. I'm sorry. How's Sam?"

"Terrified," Lyra admits, her voice soft. "He keeps saying that it's his fault 'Ms. Lady' had to go away. How the fuck could we ever let him get involved in this mess?" She clutches her forehead and leans against the counter for support, still holding the gun in her other hand. "It was supposed to be different with us, you know? We were going to break the cycle and all that shit. You were meant to end up off the streets and out of jail, and I was…" She tilts her head up toward the ceiling and sighs. "I don't know. Maybe a doctor or something. But look at us. You got your druggie girlfriend knocked up after three months of dating, nearly got your ass thrown in prison, and I got pregnant in my first semester of community college. What a pair we make, huh?"

"A pair of fucking warriors," I say. "Look at us. Life hasn't beaten us down yet."

"Yeah." She looks at me and shrugs. "I guess you could say that. Warriors or fucking nutcases."

"Either way, we stick it out," I say. "We stay together. It's always been the two of us against the world. That won't change any time soon."

"Yeah, until the world blows up with us in it. Then that doesn't sound so nice, does it?"

I shrug off the comeback and pay attention to the obvious signs underneath. All my life, Lyra has been the strong one. The sole unbreakable force in our fucked-up family, forced to shoulder even my responsibilities when my world went to shit. I never even thanked her for all she's done, but I can see the toll it's taken on her. She's hunched over the counter as if it's the only thing holding her up. Her hair is a mess, her outfit wrinkled. I can note the purple bags under her eyes, even from across the room.

"You look wrecked, Ly."

She scoffs. "Gee, thanks, Daze. It wasn't like I was up all night, worried sick about your silly ass, or anything." She pivots to face me, her expression stern. "Tell me that you understand the mess you've gotten yourself in, because I sure as hell don't."

"It's my fault," I say. "I take full responsibility. Sam never should have been involved in this shit."

"That's uncharacteristically noble of you," Lyra points out. "But it wasn't entirely your fault either. You were right. Those were the people Silas was involved with."

I nod.

She hisses through clenched teeth and punches the counter. "Fuck! Ow!" Cradling her arm against her chest, she leans against the nearest wall and sighs again. "Damn him. You'd think that when his nephew's life is on the line, he'd at least show some restraint. The fucking cocky son of a bitch. I will never forgive him for that."

"I don't think he thought Sam was ever at risk," I admit, not that I enjoy coming to the bastard's defense. "He knew I wouldn't take the chance."

"I don't give a shit what he thought." Lyra stands tall, and I've never seen her look so damn tired. "I've protected that bastard for long enough, and this is how he repays me? No more. I'm done."

"Protected..." My guard instantly goes up at the careful way she said that word. "What do you mean?"

She bites her lip and shrugs. After raking a hand through her hair, she turns her attention toward the back window overlooking the small yard and a garage.

"I mean that when you asked me about what Silas was into, I lied," she says.

I grit my teeth to remain silent. I fucking knew it. She let that bastard into her home, but just how bad was the extent of her cooperation? Trust Silas to put not only his own life at risk but everyone he claims to love as well.

"Oh, don't look at me like that," Lyra snaps. "I'm not as stupid as you think. I told him no illegal shit—he promised. But he said that any little way I could help would be helping Sam, and he's done so much for him while you were locked up—"

"Don't blame me," I snap, unable to control myself. "I warned you about that bastard. I warned you."

"I know." She looks so young standing there that I drop the anger—for now.

"Just tell me what he had you do. All of it."

"It's not like he had me drawing up heist schematics, Day. Jesus, I'm not that much of a fucking idiot."

"Then what? Just tell me now."

"He had me store some stuff for him," she admits. "Before you panic, it's not fucking drugs. I made sure of that. But otherwise, I have no idea, and I wanted to keep it that way."

"Store stuff. Lyra..." I form a fist, and it takes all the restraint I have to keep from slamming it into the wall. "What the fuck do you mean, store stuff? Don't you realize that's the oldest trick in the fucking book? Jesus Christ! If your name is tied up in any of his mess, don't you understand how that's going to look? Fuck, you could have just put your entire life on the line for that piece of shit—"

"Don't lecture me about the risks of trusting a gangbanger, alright?" she snarls. "I trusted you once, remember? And we both know how that turned out. Silas promised me that he had shit under control, and for what he paid me, I wasn't about to ask. My hours were getting cut, and the bills won't pay themselves. Not to mention that putting a kid through private preschool is fucking expensive."

"I gave you money. Whatever I could spare. Don't put this on me."

"I'm not, and I know you tried. But it wasn't enough," she shakes her head sadly. "It wasn't enough, and Silas offered to fill the gap. Besides, when he showed up with just a few boxes it didn't seem like such a bad deal to make. Don't blame me for taking him at his word. Besides, it seemed harmless enough, and he hasn't asked about it again. I bet he probably forgot he left them with me."

"Left boxes of what? Come on, Lyra, tell me you weren't that fucking stupid."

"As I said I never looked in them. I just had a friend I know in the police department do me a favor and bring a drug-sniffing dog around. It didn't so much as twitch, so whatever it is, it isn't drugs."

"But it could be weapons," I snap. "Or fucking body parts, for all you know!"

She shrugs. "Well, the dog would have picked up on that, wouldn't it?"

"Where?" I ask, fighting to keep my tone in check. "Just tell me you rented a storage shed someplace, and you weren't naïve enough to store whatever the fuck it is in your house."

She rolls her eyes in exasperation. "This is fucking rich. You think you have any right to give me the safety speech?"

"Where, Lyra?"

She inclines her head toward the window again. "I didn't let him store it in the house per se. It's out there in the garage, but it's always locked, and Sam knows better than to play around there. Besides, like I said, I doubt Silas even remembers it's there. It's been years since he left it there and he hasn't asked about it since. He just made me promise to never touch it or even look in the boxes without his permission. They're locked anyway, so it's not like I could have. I'm sure it's probably paperwork. He said they were an insurance policy—"

"And you believed him? Fuck, for all you know, there could be a bomb hidden out there!"

"Well, after the stunt he pulled, I don't feel obligated to protect him anymore, do I?" She narrows her eyes. "You can have whatever the fuck it is. I don't care."

"You can't stay here. You pack your shit, and you come with me. I'll put you up for a few days."

"And what about Sammy? You think he can just hide in a bunker and miss school for however long your little pissing contest goes on for?"

"I don't plan on it taking very long at all," I mutter.

"Daze. Tell me you aren't planning to do what I think you are. Please. Silas is a dick, but think about Sam. He wouldn't want you doing anything that could jeopardize your freedom—"

"Go pack your stuff, and I'll handle whatever the hell it is you have in the garage. But I mean it, Lyra. From now on, you have to trust me. I care about Sam more than anyone—even you," I add before she can argue. "He's all I have left, and I'll be damned if I let Silas rope him into some dangerous bull-shit. Just trust me."

"Fine, but I'm sure he has people watching the house. They probably already know you're here. I'll go pack up Sammy and the van. Then I'll get you the boxes from the garage. You think I hate you, but I don't Daze. I have always looked out for you from day one, but it's been nearly impossible to trust you. Don't let me down."

"I won't. You get your stuff, and I'll get Sam's."

I find him in the living room, watching a cartoon on low volume. He beams when he sees me and throws his arms around my waist. Then he scans the room as if hunting for someone else. "Where is Ms. Lady?" he asks. "I wanted to show her my room. Can she come and play?"

"Not right now, buddy." I crouch to his level and smooth the hair back from his face. I'll never get over just how much he looks like Renna. He may have my eyes, sure, but the innocence in his expression is all her. That enduring hope in whoever they look at, as if you're the most important fucking person in the universe, and they have no doubt about that. They'll follow you to the ends of the earth if they have to. Their love is just that fucking pure.

"Where is she?" he asks. "I want to play."

"She's... Away for a little while. You and I are gonna help get her back."

"Okay!"

"To do that, we're going to need to go on a little adventure. Would you like that?"

He nods.

"Good. Let's go pack your favorite clothes and toys."

"Okay, Daddy!" He takes my hand and leads me upstairs. I haven't been in this house in a long damn time, but his room is the largest, decorated in his favorite colors with more toys than most stores have stocked. Lyra may be a hard-ass, but I don't question for a second just how much she loves my kid. He's as much hers as he is mine, and I can't blame her for wanting the best for him.

Or at least that's what I tell myself as I shove Sam's prized belongings in a tiny suitcase and carry it out to the van. She's already waiting there, arguing with someone else who arrived just in time.

"What is this Daze?" Lyra snaps. "You think I need a fucking escort? I can drive myself."

"Ben will get you where you need to go," I say. "And he'll make sure that nothing happens along the way. Now show me where you've kept those boxes."

She heads into the backyard while I follow. I have no doubt that her suspicion is probably correct. Silas must have someone watching the house, but if one of his boys hasn't shown up yet, it could only mean one of two things.

Either what's in those boxes isn't important enough for him to give a shit about.

Or it's extremely important, enough that he needs more than one man to protect it. He needs backup.

"It's in there," Lyra says. "But I'm counting on you, Daze. Silas loves Sam, but I'm not as stupid as you think. I know what going against him means. Just make sure I don't regret it."

"You won't," I say. "Now get in the van and let Ben drive. He'll get you someplace safe, and then I'll meet up with you."

"Okay. I do love you, you crazy son of a bitch," she says, pulling me into a hug. "I do. And when it comes down to you and anyone else in the world except my kid, and Sam, you know that I will pick you every single time."

"Don't get all mushy on me now," I say, pulling back. "Just get on the road. I'll meet up with you when I can. Keep Sam safe."

She sighs, eyeing me up and down. "You never have to ask me for that. Take care of yourself, Daze."

"I very much intend to."

Standing on the curb, I watch her until the second she's in the van, and it takes off—with Ben behind the wheel—and turns the corner a few blocks away. Then I approach the garage, unsure of what the fuck I'll even find. As skeptical as I am, I doubt Silas would store anything illegal here. He has the Saints' warehouses for that and a network to funnel any shit out of the city. So, what in the hell could he want to hide in the garage of a residential neighborhood in the suburbs?

A part of me wants to suspect that it's nothing valuable. Just something small to test Lyra's willingness before he used her house to smuggle dope later down the road.

But...

The rest of me isn't quite that convinced. That part is why I'm armed with at least two weapons, just in case. Silas has the entire Saints' network to launder his dirty work, but he would only hide something in Lyra's that he wanted guarded. Something he didn't trust to keep in his own house or with any of his lackeys. Something, perhaps, he wanted to keep hidden even from Heywood himself.

And there are very few things in the world that could be.

I'm already stiffening with dread as I unlock the door and enter the dusty space. She has shit from decades ago in here. Dad's old bike. A cradle from the Stone Ages. At the very back of the room, behind an old stereo system, is a large old-fashioned military-style trunk with a key lock. I lift it, expecting it to be heavy, but it's light. Too light to be a shipment of illegal weapons, at least. Still, I'm curious the longer I stare at it and try to figure out what the hell Silas could have inside it.

He didn't leave Lyra the key. Luckily for me, she kept some tools in here apart from the museum of old memories. I find a crowbar and make short work of the lock. As I crouch to lift the lid, I start laughing to myself. After all this trouble, it would be fitting if all I found inside were some old mementos that Silas was too embarrassed to leave lying around his house. An old teddy bear or some shit. Maybe actual insurance paperwork like Lyra thought.

When I finally heft the lid open, a stack of bureaucratic documents isn't what I see. Neither is it cocaine or heroin.

In a sense, I suspect it's something far worse than all those things combined.

And it's the one tool I can use to take down Heywood.

Incredulous, all I can do is laugh louder at the sight. "Well, fuck."

I don't know what I expected. A murder weapon tied to some series of unsolved crimes? Silas' soul, for fuck's sake?

Anything but a bunch of old newspaper clippings, detailing possible cartel hits, along with a stack of documents in a folder with the Heywood name stamped onto the front. I flip through it, unsure of what I'll find. Then I spot one page in particular that makes me freeze. It looks like a fairly-new copy of a much older will. The name at the top? Abagail Heywood.

"...the bastard's already inside." The unfamiliar voice comes from outside, accompanied by a set of heavy footsteps traipsing through Lyra's overgrown garden.

Fuck. Just my luck. I could leave the documents behind, but at the last minute, I decide to tuck them under one arm while opening the door with the other hand.

From the corner of my eye, I catch movement flicker around the side of the structure. Paired with the still-advancing footsteps from the other end, I count at least two potential attackers. Apparently, Silas has his boys watching Lyra's place after all.

But why choose now to strike?

In all honesty, I don't fucking care for their reasons.

I lunge as the first motherfucker comes into view. He barely manages to choke out a grunt before I have him pinned to the ground with a knife at his throat. He gapes at me wide-eyed, scrambling to reach for his hip. I beat him to the punch, finding a pistol holstered just beneath the fall of his leather jacket.

Silas isn't playing around, it seems.

But neither am I.

Pulling the weapon free, I ram the butt of it against the bastard's skull, rendering him unconscious. Then I lurch upright and pivot just in time to catch the second punk racing from around the garage.

"You fucked up, Daze," he tells me, his face contorted in a snarl. I don't recognize him, meaning he signed up with Silas long after I left the Saints. He's even wearing our patch on the sleeve of his leather jacket, and I feel disgust wash over me. "Just leave it alone and bounce," he demands, his hands in the air. "You don't want this smoke, trust me."

"Fuck you," I counter, aiming at his head. "And fuck Silas. I'm not going to kill you, though. I want you to deliver a little message for me—I have what he's been hiding. If he wants it, he can fucking come for it."

I wait until the bastard makes the mistake of trying to reach for his own gun. Then I do pull the trigger, striking him in the leg. He slumps over, howling like a goddamn animal, but I only pause long enough to pick up his gun from where it fell and take off through the alley before one of Lyra's neighbors calls the cops.

Somehow, I managed to keep the documents tucked under my arm all this time, but I feel a growing sense of dread at the prospect of discovering just what they contain.

Namely, why in the hell is Silas interested in Frey?

EIGHT

FREY

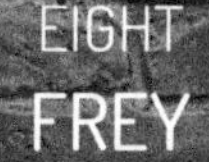

I'M WORRIED. The guards have left me alone for hours this time, without even the customary sandwich or trip to the bathroom—a bad sign. Despite my full bladder, I am not the slightest bit relieved when I hear footsteps finally approach. In fact, I feel more like a soldier on D-day, grimly resigned to the horror I might face in the moments ahead. How I react will not only determine my own life and freedom but the welfare of every person I care about.

There is no turning back. No time to rethink my only course of action. The razor blade is already in my grasp, and all I can do next is act.

And pray.

I've already made peace with what I must do to avoid being dragged to some creepy altar—because if I let myself be taken beyond this dingy room, there won't be any meaningful future for me afterward.

I'm ready.

As the doorknob turns, I still feel a sick, heavy dread settle in my stomach as I rise to the balls of my feet. I step forward as the figure pushes the door wider, all while manipulating the blade between my fingertips. There's no time to think. No room to second-guess. Lunge! I tell myself as a slender figure steps into the doorway, serving as my only obstacle to escape.

It should be Colton, his expression contorted in a cruel, menacing sneer.

Not...

"C-Catherine." I barely manage to tuck my hand behind my back before she can see the razor blade. As a result, it bites deep into the flesh of my palm. Damn it! I just hope it didn't break the skin. Fighting to keep my expression blank, I croak out, "What are you doing here?"

"Hello." Her voice is as welcoming as always, though her smile resembles more of a grimace than anything joyful. My apprehension only grows as I crane my neck to fully take her in. For once, she's slacked on her primary duty of being Michael Heywood's polished, perfect wife always. The illusion has cracked. Her eyes are sunken, her hair a lifeless and dull mass coiled into a low bun. She's wearing one of the outfits my father insists she be seen in public in, but it's ill-fitting, practically swallowing her narrow frame. In only the past few days, she's lost an alarming amount of weight.

"It's so good to see you, Frances," she says softly. I can tell from how her eyes widen that she's as shocked by my appearance as I am by hers. Self-consciously, I start to smooth my filthy skirt, not that it will do any good. Nothing can hide the bruises covering my body from head to toe.

"Michael thought that you would like it if I helped you get ready," Catherine explains. Despite her gaze darting around the room, I can't tell if she's shocked that I've been held here for so long.

Watching her chips away at the steely resolve I've built up since Silas left. God, the razor blade in my grasp seems to burn, demanding to be used. But could I really attack Catherine? I want so badly to lump her into the same category as my father and Colton, but...

It's not fair. The concept of freedom seems so fragile, drifting further out of my reach with each passing second. All I have to do is stick to my plan and seize the moment.

But I don't have Daze's fighting spirit and his fierce ability to remain focused.

I'm weaker, prone to pathetic second-guessing—like the fact that Catherine never harmed me once. Though she's married to my father, I don't have any ill will toward her, either. I'm sure he knows that, and he sent her here in his stead on purpose.

To keep me from doing anything rash that might disrupt his meticulous planning.

In response to Catherine's expectant stare, all I can muster up is a single, breathless question. "Why?"

"I'm going to go with you to the wedding venue," she says, avoiding the question directly. "Your dress is already there, and it's so pretty, Frances. I know you'll like it." Tentatively, she reaches out and fingers a long tendril of my hair with another strained, labored smile.

I duck out of her reach. "Are we going back to the house?" I ask, feeling my hope rise. That could be a better location in the end than here. I know the area well enough, at least, to find an escape without potentially resorting to violence. Maybe this will all work out for the best?

"No, Frances," Catherine says as she slowly shakes her head. My heart sinks. "Not at the house."

There's no point in hiding my confusion. "Then where?"

She pats my shoulder, still forcing that painful grin. "Let's not worry about that now. Have you been eating okay?"

I nod. It's obvious that this isn't some charming weekend away. Even though she appears exhausted and haggard, I look just as bad, if not worse. If I had some hope squirreled away that Catherine might resist my father's antics, then her pretend act now thoroughly dashes them. She's determined to play along, no matter the cost.

And yet, I still can't force myself to raise the razor blade.

"I'm fine," I choke out, instead.

"Good," she says weakly before taking my free hand. "Good."

We leave the church and approach a van driven by an unfamiliar man in black. There, I realize the first of many precautions my father is willing to take to keep me in line.

And to keep Daze and his cohorts from even dreaming of a rescue.

My guard goes up even before Catherine uses her narrow body to block my view while she lifts something from the seat.

"I'm sorry," she says, her voice breaking, as she turns to me while holding the item in question—a long, thin strip of black fabric. "He insisted. I'm so sorry. I don't even know how to—" She bites off her words and tries again. "I'm so sorry. I won't tie it too tight. I promise."

As Catherine ties the blindfold around the back of my head, blocking out the gray daylight, I'm too exhausted to feel dread or even hopelessness. If I've learned nothing during the past few weeks, it's that there's no use in crying over spilled milk or dwelling on the seemingly inevitable future. All I can do is focus on the present and be ready for the next chance to seize my freedom.

Speaking of... I remember the razor blade still in my palm. As Catherine ushers me inside, I have no choice. I can't tuck it into my skirt while blinded, and I certainly can't risk her seeing it out in the open. As I sense her enter behind me, I do the only thing I can.

I pretend to cough and shove it into my mouth, narrowly avoiding slicing my tongue. Powered by adrenaline, I manage to sit while concealing the weapon against the inside of my cheek.

Unfortunately, Catherine, not one for chatty conversation normally, seems determined to fill the silence now. "I'm sure you'll love the dress," she chirps once she's seated beside me, and the van starts moving beneath me. "It's lace and has a beautiful design, and I know the veil will be very special to you. It was your mother's," she says hesitantly. "I badgered Michael until he let me take it out of storage. I know she would have wanted you to wear it, even if he insisted that it be dyed—"

"How do you know what she would have wanted?" Even with the razor precariously pressed against my inner cheek, I can't help the vitriol that spills out of me—as a harsh snarl, I barely recognize. Burning hot tears spill from my eyes, wetting the fabric obscuring my vision. I'm clenching my jaw, recklessly ignoring the sharpened strip of metal pressed against tender, sensitive flesh. "You didn't know her. You didn't know the first damn thing about her!"

"You're right," Catherine says softly after a few moments of silence. "I'm sorry for mentioning it. I had no right. You deserve to be angry with me. I really am so sorry."

Instead of responding, I turn my attention to the drive. Whenever we are, it's out of the city. I can feel the road switch from smooth asphalt to the rough, rugged country roads that line the outskirts of the city limits. As far as I know, there's nothing out this way for miles. Certainly not a church.

Just where is my father planning to hold this wedding? At least one of his aims is clear—he wants it somewhere that Daze could never find.

To calm my nerves, I count down the passing minutes. Then, the hours. One. Two...

Any hope I had of a last-minute Daze rescue vanishes. Without allies, I'm alone.

While it feels like a cold comfort, I can't deny that there is nothing more reassuring than having a weapon on me. When I swallow, the telltale scrape reminds me of the danger I'm in and what's really at stake. Colton seemed to be envisioning a future far different than the one my father had in store. Sooner or later, they are in for a collision, and I need to make sure that I am far, *far* away when their fragile alliance finally crumbles.

Suddenly, Catherine shifts beside me, alluding to a change in the monotony. "Finally," she mutters. "We're almost there. It won't be very long now."

There is a pause, as if the property we're entering is blocked by some kind of gate or path, requiring the driver to stop. I swear I can hear old, metal hinges creaking as I strain my ears. There aren't many places near Westpoint City that have such an approach. But where? Abruptly, the van lurches forward again, and all my focus goes to staying upright in my seat.

Beneath us, the road becomes coarse and riddled with what must be rocks that jostle me and Catherine from side to side. I can barely keep my balance. As the van suddenly pitches to the right, I'm thrown directly into Catherine.

As my cheek bounces off her shoulder, my stomach sinks through the floor. Dear God, no. Fiery pain lances through my jaw, and warm, hot liquid floods my mouth in a seemingly never-ending stream. *Don't panic*, I tell myself. *Just breathe. Swallow. Don't panic.*

"I hate this drive," Catherine exclaims, oblivious to my injury. "I can't wait until I can show you inside. I'm sure you'll love it, and even if it isn't the wedding you envisioned, I've worked hard to make it as beautiful as possible. You'll see."

All I can do is nod as my cheek sears, on fire. I can feel part of the razor still embedded in the skin. Damn it. There is no other choice but for me to manually free it. As blood threatens to dribble down my chin, I panic and press my hand to my mouth in a pathetic bid to buy more time.

"Are you okay?" Catherine asks, sounding closer. Her voice shakes, but I can't tell if her unease is due to nerves or shock.

"No," I say thickly. "I think I bit my tongue." Speaking at all is excruciating, and I can only pray that I don't somehow swallow the razor entirely before I can free it.

Though, in a sick, morbid twist of irony, that would certainly end my ordeal and thwart my father's plans in one fell swoop.

Daze wouldn't approve, though. Thinking of him must change my entire demeanor, because Catherine exclaims in alarm.

"Oh no! Let's get you to a bathroom." She takes my free hand and guides me forward, presumably from the van. I struggle to interpret my surroundings as my feet contact what feels like a gravel-strewn path. The air here is cool, devoid of any sounds that serve as hallmarks of Westpoint City. Chirping birds sing to each other, and lonely wind rustles what sounds like swaying trees. Despite the flood of information, I still have no idea where we are as I'm hastened up a set of rickety steps that squeal with every movement, but I can tell the second we enter yet another enclosed space. A house, maybe? The air itself changes, becoming thick and suffocating. Under the blindfold, sweat slicks my forehead, weighing down my matted hair.

"It's this way," Catherine explains while hurriedly guiding me along what seems like winding corridors. After pulling me to a stop, she gently unties my blindfold. As I blink to make sense of my surroundings, her constricted expression comes into focus first. "Oh dear."

Her horrified gasp adds a new concern to my rapidly worsening bleeding—though I could hemorrhage to death for all I care. Above all, I can't let her see the razor.

"Open your mouth," she says, turning to a porcelain sink in what I quickly realize is a spacious, if old-fashioned, bathroom. "Oh dear. I hope you didn't bite too deeply—"

"No!" I push past her and crouch over a clawfoot bathtub. Under the guise of testing my tongue, I press the tip of my finger against the side of the blade. Holy crap. It's in deeper than I thought. My fingers shake as I attempt to use two to pry it free. Wet with blood, they slide uselessly along the sharpened surface. When I finally pull it out, I barely manage to crush it in a fist as Catherine comes up beside me.

"Oh, what a mess," she says, tsking her tongue. "You poor thing. Maybe we should call a doctor or something—"

"I'm fine," I say, swiping at my mouth with the sleeve of my shirt. It comes away red.

"You're not," Catherine insists, her tone unusually firm. "I wish Michael would postpone. I don't even know why he's insisting that it happen tonight..." She trails off, and I turn to find her staring into space, her jaw clenched. In an instant, she transforms from the ideal trophy wife to a woman more suitable of her age. Woefully young and out of her element.

I leave her to it and press a rag to my mouth while scanning the room we're in. It's well-maintained but obviously disused. The silver fixtures and hand-painted wallpaper resemble the kind of finery on display in the prestigious family manors of my father's wealthier patrons, Colton's family, the Abernathys, included. In fact, I wonder if we're on one of their properties. From what I remember, they had several, spread throughout the nearby countryside. The only catch is that I have no idea which ones may be located several hours outside of the city.

"Where are we?" I ask Catherine directly, taking a risk.

She whips around to face me as if she's forgotten I was even there. One look at her wary expression, and I'm sure she'll refuse to answer. Instead, she glances at the closed door and then twitches in my direction as if she has to stop herself from whispering directly into my ear.

"The old Abernathy estate," she murmurs, confirming my suspicion. "It's been in their family for generations. Michael thought it might be fitting to have the wedding here, but..." She bites her bottom lip, and her slender shoulders seem to deflate beneath the unspoken secret of what my father truly has in store. "I think I would have preferred it at home, at least. Where you could be comfortable and have your friends."

"He said it would be tonight," I say, wincing as the inside of my cheek stings. "Do you know what time?"

She shakes her head. "I'm not sure. After the others arrive, I'm sure."

"The others?" I tense at the wording, even more worried, when she glances away. "Who? What do you mean?"

"We should get you cleaned up." She gently takes the rag from me and attempts to dab at my damp jaw.

I evade her reach. "Look at me," I demand.

"Frances, let's not waste any more time than we already have. Please." Through another pretty, strained smile, I can clearly see the fear she can't hide. Her hands shake as she wrings them together over her ill-fitting dress. With every slight sound to come from the hall, she jumps. It's as though she's convinced my father is lurking behind the door, listening to every word she says.

She isn't merely worried—she's terrified.

"Who?" I ask again, my voice softer. "Who are the others?"

"Frances, please." She fiddles with the rag as if blind to the blood already staining it. "I can't. I can't—"

"I need to know what's happening."

She shakes her head and tries to shrug me off. "No. We should go see your dress. You're going to love—"

"Stop it!" While concealing the blade in my other hand, I grab her wrist firmly, and I don't bother to sound gentle anymore. "Listen to me! You know what this is, don't you?"

She flinches and shakes her head more earnestly. "Frances, I think we should—"

"Don't you? Answer me!"

"I..."

"I don't want to be here," I snarl, wrenching away from her. "You can see that. This isn't what I want. My father is forcing me to marry Colton, and I need to know why. Or are you willing to just stand aside and watch me be destroyed the same way you failed Hale?"

"Don't." Her face pales, and a coldness falls over her gaze that I've never seen before. Suddenly, she seems years older. Decades.

"You think I wanted that to happen?" she asks hoarsely. "You think I wanted Hale to die? I tried to warn him! I tried. Much like you, he wouldn't listen. What happened to him wasn't my fault!"

"I need your help now," I say. "Please. Tell me what's going on so that I'm not walking in there blind like some lamb to the slaughter."

She grimaces and holds out the rag. "Please, just let me help you clean up first. Please."

I submit to having her wipe my face of blood, all the while, the razor is biting into my palm. The thought of using it crosses my mind fleetingly, but I don't even entertain the idea seriously. Once my face is cleaned to her liking, Catherine moves to sit on the rim of the bathtub. Dressed in a pale-blue sundress, with her hair hanging loosely down her shoulders, it strikes me just how well she's played her role all these years. Michael Heywood's pure, doting wife who possessed none of the flaws that my mother did.

Deep down, I always resented her for that. She made it look so easy, standing in my father's shadow. The truth is, I never paid close enough attention to see just how much of a toll the ruse was taking on her. She's a shadow of a woman, weighed down by her neat costume. For the first time in years, as I settle onto the floor, I finally catch glimpses of the real woman lurking beneath the mask. Even from this angle, she seems pitifully small.

"You think that this is all to punish you, I'm sure," she says, her voice barely audible. "It's not. We are but pawns in a much larger game. I'm sure that Michael wouldn't even acknowledge our existence unless he was forced to."

"Forced," I echo, tasting the word. "How do you mean?"

For the umpteenth time, her eyes dart to the doorway, but when they return to me, I notice a steely resolve that wasn't there before. It gives her the strength to sit straighter with her head held high, and further fractures the mask of Michael Heywood's wife.

"You know what I mean," she says. "You aren't the only one here under duress, and I know it's hard for you, Frances. I do." She slips from the rim of the tub to her knees and cradles both of my hands against her lap. I barely manage to tighten my fist to ensure the blade is hidden from view—though it is the least alarming detail regarding my fingers. They're still coated in fresh blood, as is the once pristine skirt of Catherine's pretty dress. There is no indication that she cares or even notices.

"You think you're the only one forced to conform to his wishes? You aren't. You think I stood aside and let Hale die with a simpering smile on my face, but it is far from the truth..." Her voice breaks and her fingers grip mine tightly as she draws in a steadying breath. "You may not believe me, but I tried to help him. In my own way, I *did*."

I give one of her hands a reassuring squeeze. "Then help me. You can do that right now. Just help me get out of here."

"I can't," she insists. "I mean it. The place is surrounded. If I speak too loudly, Michael's men will be here in a heartbeat. You have no idea the pressure he's been under. The things he's been into to secure his election... I saw them in the barn, and God, I didn't want to believe that he could—"

"What?" I press as she trails off. "Tell me."

She sighs. "You know I can't."

I don't know why I'm so disappointed—but I am. "Fine," I snap, rising to my feet. "Then just take me to my cell until the wedding—"

"But I can show you," she whispers as if I'd never spoken. Tilting her head back, she watches me silently before lurching upright. As she approaches the door, she whispers over her shoulder, "Follow my lead and keep your eyes downcast. We have an hour before Michael and the others arrive. Just... Stay close to me."

She tosses the used rag aside and pries open the door, peeking beyond it for one of my father's men. I assume a guard is nearby because I hear her cheerfully say, "The poor thing bit her tongue on the ride over and got blood all over herself. We need to use the big sink in the kitchen to get her cleaned up. Is that okay?"

The guard must give her the go-ahead because she reaches for my hand and pulls me along.

"This way."

I do my best to keep my head down while taking in every inch of the place that I can. As far as figurative prisons go, it's a step up from the windowless back room of the church, but far less inviting. From the faded décor and dated furniture we pass, it's obvious that Catherine hadn't been lying about where we are, at least. It looks like the sort of dusty museum to old money that a family as wealthy as Colton's would maintain long after its heyday if only for the status symbol of it all.

Surprisingly, that doesn't narrow down any potential locations. It never occurred to me to pay attention when he waxed poetic about his family's many estates. Focusing on where I am won't do any good either way. My sole concern now should be finding a way out.

The place is huge, and I note a large guard presence. Catherine was right. I can feel several pairs of watchful eyes tracking our every movement past a dusty drawing room and into a narrow kitchen. There, Catherine rushes to close the door, muttering something sweetly about privacy. The second the door slams shut, she takes my hand in a bruising grip, her voice low.

"We only have a few minutes. Listen to every word I say, and don't question."

The unusual sternness in her gaze convinces me to nod.

"Good. Now get on your knees and crawl." She points to the far wall of the space, past a large fridge.

"W-What?"

"Please, hurry!" She tugs on my wrist, urging me to my knees over the polished, though worn, marble tile beneath us. "That way," she whispers. "Don't make any noise. Just do it." At the same time, she flips on the water faucet and raises her voice, her tone jovial. "Oh, you've sure made a mess. We'll have to wash your hair, you poor thing—" From over her shoulder, she once again glances at the wall.

Taking care to make as little noise as I can over the creaking floor, I inch in that direction, still clutching the razor blade against my palm. It feels like an eternity before I finally reach the row of cupboards. At a glance I don't find anything even remotely worth the secrecy.

Peeking my way again, Catherine motions for me to open the nearest cupboard. I do and find what must have been an old laundry chute with a latch in the floor. When I look back at Catherine, she mimes lifting the lid, and mouths, "Slowly."

I obey, struggling to move the heavy lid without making too much noise. Beneath it is a dark void that must extend all the way to the lower level. I can't make out anything in the pitch darkness.

But I can smell. Is that…

Sweat, musk, and unmentionable substances that could only come from human beings crammed into one place for an extended amount of time. A chill runs down my spine and I have to consciously remember to lower the lid quietly. Still, I'm sure I make more noise than necessary as I leap to my feet and back away from that cupboard as quickly as I can.

"Oh dear, these stains just don't want to budge," Catherine says, still babbling to herself. "Let me try some soap."

Taking a handful, she smears it on my dress, then washes off the remaining stains with water. As a knock rattles the door, her hands shake.

"Just a minute!"

"Mr. Heywood requests your presence, Miss."

"Oh, of course. We'll be out soon!" Her eyes frantically meet mine as she rushes to make it appear as if all this time, we'd been cleaning me up. By the time Catherine finally pulls the door open, my hair is dripping wet, and my dress is soaked.

The guard standing on the other end looks me over before beckoning us both toward the end of the hall with a nod. "He's waiting for you in the drawing room, Miss."

"Okay, I'll be right there after I show Frances to her room—"

"He wants to see you both," the guard says. "This way."

NINE

DAZE

IF ANYONE HAD TOLD me a few days ago that I would not only be hiding out in a former cartel stronghold but *working* with the bastards, I would have said they were crazy. The sick son of a bitch might even have deserved a punch to the gut for such a twisted idea.

Well, look at me now.

I'd skip down the street hand-in-hand with the devil if it meant saving Frey's life. *Liar*, a part of me whispers. If you truly cared about her... *Really* cared, you'd pass over the devil and go straight to Silas on your hands and knees. You'd offer the bastard your head on a silver platter if it meant getting her back alive.

After that, you'd ask why he had so many documents pertaining to her family tucked away in a suburban garage. That's a tricky little riddle, I have yet to solve. Hours later and I still haven't gone through them all—for a reason that isn't entirely my fault. When Damien saw the folder the second I returned, he frowned in that mysterious way that signals bad news.

I'd almost prefer to ask Silas outright than dig answers out of Mayhem, though, the bastard would sooner blow my brains out—after he stopped laughing his ass off, that is. Still, the doubt persists at the back of my mind, in between taunting images of her. The beautiful green eyes that widened as I fucked her last. Skin so soft, and as pure as an angel's. Right before an orgasm, her voice rose in pitch, and I swear it must be the soundtrack those lucky bastards arrive to in real fucking heaven.

Damn.

This is one of the few times in my life where constantly thinking about a woman isn't a good thing. I'm not used to this. *Pining,* as Ben would call it, his voice teasing—and rightfully so. My fear of losing her has grown from a minor inconvenience into full-blown paranoia. She consumes my thoughts. Even with Renna...

I knew she was in a bad way, but by the time Sammy came, whatever there had been between us had already died out. We were glorified roommates, tethered together by a screaming infant neither of us was responsible enough to care for. Yes, I felt grief when she died, and it might be shitty of me to admit, but...I felt relief, too. There was no need to worry about her shooting up or nodding off with Sam in the house.

That being said, I missed her. But, when it came to saying goodbye, as much as it fucking sucked, I could let her go.

The possibility of losing Frey isn't even an option. There's no alternative to having her back in my arms. No happy ending that doesn't involve her in it. Being away from her kills me.

Truth is, I would go further than meeting with the cartel if I knew she would be safe. I'd sell my soul for her.

"I don't like this," Ben murmurs, hunched over the table, comparing pages from Hale's journal to those in Silas' trunk. In the pale glow filtering in from the high windows, he looks like hell, with his dark hair hanging limply down his shoulders and his chin coated in black stubble. "There's news clippings of the cartel mingled with a fucking last will and testament—"

"What?" I approach the other end of the table as he shoves one of the pages toward me. My stomach twists into knots as I scan the wording printed in faded ink. It's a will, alright, documenting the final wishes of one Abagail Winston Heywood.

"She might have been Frey's mother," I say, recalling what she told me about her. "Supposedly, she was a drug addict, but Heywood more than likely bumped her off."

"This could be why," Ben says, nodding toward the stack of pages still on his side of the table. "Looks like Ms. Abby here was worth millions. I'm talking *tens* of millions. I can't tell the full amount because these are copies of just a few pages. Why the hell Silas would have it, I don't know."

"What else is there? Maybe he's threatening to release this to the press? The knowledge that he's riding high on his ex-wife's money could erode his financial support?"

"Maybe," Ben says. At the same time, he frowns and presses his thumb over a particular line. "If he actually *did* ride high on her money. Judging from this, he didn't."

I feel my eyes narrow. Fuck, I'm even more confused. Why would Silas even give a damn, unless...

"I'm guessing that if Heywood didn't profit from his wife's death, then her children did."

"Not quite." Ben sighs, but when he meets my gaze, he's frowning. "Hale would have when he turned twenty-five."

"So, then I'm guessing Frey is next in line."

And since she's only twenty-three, she has two years on her father's radar before she can inherit. Not ideal, but I plan on getting her out of the city well before then. Even so, something about the way Ben is looking at me makes my skin itch.

"What?"

"She is next in line to inherit, but it looks like there are exceptions built in. Either she inherits when she's twenty-five, or if she gets married and has a child before then."

I blink at him. Hell, he might as well have punched me in the chest. Marriage. A child. "For all we know Heywood could have her married to his fucking puppet by now." I take off toward the entrance. What the hell I'll do? Who knows.

All that matters is getting her far from those monsters.

"Wait," Ben calls out. "You got any idea why Silas would keep this shit hidden like some kind of fucked-up security blanket? Or why he's been keeping tabs on the cartel in addition to Heywood's financials?"

It's a good damn question. Gritting my teeth, I stop short and force myself to meet Ben's questioning stare. I know what he's getting at. In spite of his apparent confusion, he hasn't asked any of the cartel holdouts for assistance. It is no secret that he disapproves of their presence. He'd rather we do things the old way, as my father did—go it alone under the glory of the Saints, armed with hopes and dreams.

In the long run, we'll all be better off if he gets it through his skull sooner rather than later—I'm not him.

"Why don't we ask the experts," I suggest, heading toward the back of the warehouse.

There, I find three of the five cartel holdouts seated, surrounded by cigar smoke. In the background, faint sounds of Latin pop play, providing an ironically jaunty backdrop to the tension thickening the air. They've been mostly quiet since setting up last night.

One of them, Marco, smirks when he sees me approach.

"It's about damn time you've come to make introductions," he says, cracking his knuckles before extending his hand for me to shake. "Otherwise, I might take our welcome as a sign that we aren't wanted around here."

"No disrespect intended," I say coldly. "I'm sure you've been listening to what we've been talking about over there. Any idea why those incidents would catch Heywood's eye?"

Or Silas', for that matter.

Marco laughs. "I'm no fucking psychic."

He reaches for his pocket, and I can't form a fist fast enough.

"Easy," he says with another forced laugh. "You always walk around your so-called *base* so amped up?"

"Yeah, well, I'm not fucking stupid. What's in the pocket?"

"It's this." He pulls something from his pocket, but it's not a gun. Instead, it's a card that he places on the edge of the table, forcing me to inch closer to read it. Stamped over the front in red print are the letters E.D. and what looks like a skull dribbling blood-red ink down the front of the black cardstock. "Have you heard of El Diablo?"

I raise an eyebrow. "No. Should I have?"

He shrugs. "Only if you like learning about crazy fuckers on the outskirts of the cartel. A man that even we don't work with. He deals in heroin, but it's brutal stuff. Deadly. That's not why he has the reputation that he does, though."

I relax a fraction, still keeping all three men in sight. For now, they keep their hands on the table, in clear view.

"Fine, I'll bite. How does this El Diablo get his reputation?"

"Diablo means devil," Marco explains. "According to some, this bastard is him, in the flesh. Or worships him at least."

I have to laugh. Between this shit and Heywood, I've had enough of religion to last a lifetime. "I don't care if he worships a fucking unicorn," I snap. "What does he have to do with Heywood?"

"You wanted me to look into that drug that's been flooding the market. While it's been shipped here using cartel networks, we don't deal in it. To get that stuff directly your Heywood had to literally make a deal with the devil. There are only a few things that El Diablo will accept as collateral. Money isn't one of them."

"Then what is?"

"Stop standing there like a dumbass, and we can discuss this like men."

"Fine." I approach the table and pull up the only empty chair. As I sit, I keep my stance open, ready to spring into action at a moment's notice. For now, the men don't seem eager to move. "Keep talking."

"El Diablo deals in bodies. Men. Women. Children. Doesn't matter the type, only that they're alive."

"For the sex trade?" I ask, sick at the idea.

Marco shakes his head. "Men who deal in that side of the trade don't take druggies or the old or sick. El Diablo will take anyone and everyone, as long as they won't be missed. Rarely are his victims seen again."

"For what?"

"No one knows for sure," he says. "Some think as slaves to work the cocoa fields. Other thinks that he might brainwash them all to join his cult. I've heard some other theories, though."

"And what is that?"

"Sacrifice," Marco says. "Like the Aztecs used to. He rips out the beating heart from their chest and burns it on a pyre."

"You're shitting me."

"Maybe." He shrugs. "But rumor has it that El Diablo has been moving his cult north."

I don't like the sound of that. "To the city?" I ask.

He shrugs again. "Perhaps. The point is, El Diablo never moves. In the thirty years that he's been trafficking drugs, he's never so much as left his commune. If he's here, it can't be good."

"So, Heywood, who thinks himself some kind of fucking cult prophet, has teamed up with some drug dealer who worships the devil," I say. "You couldn't write this shit. Am I really supposed to believe it?"

"Believe it. Don't believe it," Marco replies. "But there is one thing you should know. In the village where El Diablo lives now, do you want to know how he established his roots? He kidnapped a quarter of the town and killed the captives, one by one, and left their bodies to rot in the street. No one could stop him. No one dared to challenge him. And for thirty years, he's operated out of that commune without even the fucking military daring to challenge him. If he was thinking of expanding, don't doubt that he would have the resources to. And he wouldn't aim to just settle for a piece of this place. He'd take it all and drive out anyone who got in his way. Westpoint would be reduced to a shell, and if he had the fucking political darling on his side, along with the police commissioner? Who the hell knows what he could be capable of."

"Let's say I believe you. What would Heywood get out of it? Why even take the risk of ruling the city with some outsider?"

"Why else? Power and money. He gets to set up in a new, more powerful city in a new, more powerful country. The cartel already has ties in the police department. If he can make the mayor his puppet, there is no telling where his influence may end."

"But there has to be more to it," I insist. "Something big enough that Heywood is willing to put his life on the line. Already, there have been bodies found. How long does he think they can keep this up?"

"Ah, but you seem to think that they didn't want those bodies to be found. You don't see the city in a panic, do you? What if they weren't mistakes, but intentionally placed decoys?"

"To distract from what?"

"That's the real question." He sits forward, lacing his fingers together. "You should ask yourself why these rumors are coming to light now. If a man wanted to take over the city, he wouldn't want bodies being found or rumors taking root until well into his plans, right?"

"So, you're saying that we're already at the end game. Let me guess, that's when your big baddie comes to town and starts ripping out hearts?"

"Oh, you don't want him here," Marco warns. "If I were you, I'd stop him from ever setting foot in this city. If he's already on the move, then you don't have much time."

"Okay, so if you're so smart, tell me when this is all going down."

"Soon," he says with a grimace. "Maybe even tonight. I know where they'll be gathering, but you need to do the grunt work of getting inside."

"Why should I? What's even in it for you? Let me guess, you're telling me all this out of the goodness of your heart?"

"No. My sister went missing a few weeks ago. She was always a fuck up, so I didn't think much of it, at first. But she liked to run her mouth and piss the wrong people off. If she wound up in this mess... I need to know."

I look him in the eye to gauge his honesty. As the seconds pass, he doesn't so much as flinch, and I have my answer. When it comes to this, at least, he isn't lying.

But there is something that he's holding back.

"What aren't you telling me?"

Marco smiles. "You seem like the reckless, hardheaded type who runs into danger without a second thought. Do you really want to be bogged down with the finer details?"

I wince. He has a point. If it weren't for Ben, I'd be relying on just my instincts and sheer damn luck. But he's right. I can't let myself get caught up without weighing every option. It's not just my life on the line anymore.

"I have the time," I say. "So, what are these 'finer details' that you've been dancing around?"

"My men know that there's some kind of event they're planning for tonight. Something big. If El Diablo is in or near the city, he'll show for that. Which is bad news for anyone that you think they have their sights set on."

An event. Like a fucking wedding? I see red, and for a second, it's harder to remember Ben's advice. I don't want to be patient and thoughtful where Frey's life is concerned. I want to fight. Maim. Kill if I have to.

I want her safe.

I need her to be...

As if Ben is exerting his influence even from the other side of the building, I feel some sense slam back into me. What I need to be doing now is staying focused.

"Where?"

"That's the problem. I don't have an exact location, just educated guesses, but the real danger comes from the fact that I know this place will be armed to the teeth. Getting in will be a suicide mission. Could be better to wait it out and see if you can spot El Diablo."

But time isn't on our side, and there's no way in hell I'll sit aside, and watch Frey marry someone else.

"That's not all," Marco adds. "There has been an uptick of people disappearing from homeless shelters. Usual customers who have vanished."

"Let me guess, more rumors?"

"Ah, but I haven't told you the best, most salacious one of them all." Marco crosses his arms over his chest and leans in. In the dim lighting, his eyes fucking glow, and I feel like some dumb kid, listening to a ghost story. "They say that to honor his presence, El Diablo would demand a sacrifice. A grand display to show that his loyalty has been appreciated."

Sacrifice. I think of Frey with some bastard ripping out her beating heart.

"Jesus Christ. But that's just a bullshit rumor, right?"

Marco shrugs. "Who the hell knows. But if you want to go after them, we need to move now."

"Give me the locations. I'll handle this with a team of men. We can sneak past their defenses somehow—"

"You don't think I brought you here just to sip tea and for the pleasant conversation, did you?" Marco says. "Oh no, pretty boy. You're taking me with you. I need to see this shit for myself firsthand."

I raise an eyebrow at that. "So, you can kiss the ring of your creepy ass rival?"

"No. So I can see for myself if the rumors are true. If they are, you might find yourself with more allies, biker. No one wants this kind of weird bullshit in our city. If not stopped, we'll all wind up on that altar, one after the other."

He has a point. Only a fool would turn down more willing hands. At the same time, the offer sounds too good to be true. There has to be a catch lurking somewhere. Am I desperate enough to ignore the danger for now?

Maybe.

"How does that saying go?" I rasp. "Never look a gift horse in the mouth."

"Then it looks like we have a deal." Marco extends his hand.

And I have no fucking choice but to take it.

By the evening, the warehouse no longer looks like a refuge for the homeless. Within a few hours, Damien and his boys have moved equipment in, and our ragtag band is performing various tasks like some demented boy scout troop.

"Lex thinks he made headway on your missing reporter," Damien calls out once he's finished unloading a black crate filled with weapons. "I'm sure your buddy will want us to be subtle and do shit all stealth-like—" He nods toward Ben, who scoffs and waves him off. "But I'm down for a rougher introduction."

"There isn't time for games," Ben warns. "Shit's gonna get real soon, and we won't have a lot of time to fuck around. What the golden boy here—" He jerks his chin in my direction, "—has signed us up for is basically a suicide mission."

Knowing Damien, there's no need to go into the specifics. All I have to ask is, "You in?"

He grins, his teeth bared. "Hell, yes."

"Ah, but that's before he mentions the cannibal aspect."

Damien raises an eyebrow. "Seems like you've been having more fun in this city than you let on."

"Unfortunately, it's not a joke," I admit. That makes every man in the nearby radius turn his head in our direction. "Looks like our dear preaching politician got himself involved in way more than we thought. We gotta find where they are tonight."

Before it's too late for Frey.

"And I'm assuming that this mission is why three men from the cartel have just driven up to the gate?"

"The fuck?" Ben rushes to the tangled array of security monitors connected to cameras affixed outside. "Shit, Day! Those fuckers are trying to box us in! It's a trap."

"No," I say, watching as one familiar figure steps from the car at the head of the mini convoy. "It's a truce."

"What?" Ben is left sputtering as I head outside to meet Marco. "Day, what the fuck are you talking about? You didn't mention anything about working with them."

"Because I knew you wouldn't like it, but if this is what it takes to get Frey back. Then fuck it."

"What about working with the reporter, you know? What she actually wanted you to do."

He has a point.

"Then you take the lead with them. The leader's name is Marco. I'll try to pin down the fucking reporter and see what he knows, but I'll be back in time tonight, so keep me updated."

"Damn it, Day..." Ben sighs. "You don't pay me enough for this shit. Hell, you don't pay me at all!"

"You're a good man, Ben. The best anyone could ever ask for in a friend."

"Yeah, yeah, you owe me for this, you son of a bitch."

He's right, and I don't take that lightly.

Sooner or later, everything is going to come to a head, and I'm running out of promises to make.

The funny thing is that the only one that feels impossible to keep is the one I made to her.

Trust her.

But if I give her any more time, I might lose her forever.

And that's just not a risk I'm willing to take.

MY FATHER DEMANDS to see us both.

Despite the wide-eyed glance we share, Catherine hides any fear by throwing her head back and plastering on a more convincing fake smile than any I've seen before.

"Let's go." Poised with graceful confidence, she leads me into a sparsely-furnished room I vaguely remember passing on the way to the kitchen—only now, the air feels heavier. Colder. I'm shivering even before I cross the threshold, and within seconds, I have an answer as to why. Standing near a large window, with his hands clasped, eyes on the view, is my father. He doesn't even turn to acknowledge our arrival. In contrast, he tilts his head sharply at Catherine as though she were an errant fly.

"Leave us," he commands, his voice like a whip.

She lurches on the tips of her toes and nearly trips in her rush to the door. "Of course." With a curt nod, she scurries off, leaving me alone at the mouth of the room.

With her gone, I can't escape the childish urge to run and hide. At the other end of the hallway, I can make out an ornate door with a man standing guard beside it, presumably, it leads to an exit. I tell myself it wouldn't be hard to slip past him with or without the razor blade. Playing out this hypothetical scenario in my head, I imagine myself running from this place straight to Daze's arms.

Children, however, live in fictional worlds. Resigned to my current reality, I face my father without flinching, watching him relish in the fact that he has me trapped. The only trace of emotion I can see in his eyes is a malicious gleam.

"Tonight, will be your last moments as a free woman, Frances," he declares, his voice deep and rasping. He might as well be giving a sermon to thousands rather than speaking to his only daughter. Ordinarily, I would clam up and obey any command he threw my way.

Not anymore.

"Until I marry Colton, you mean," I say. It hurts to speak, and I'm sure there's still blood on my face despite Catherine's best attempts to clean me up. Good. I want him to see what he's done to me—but if I expect to find any guilt cross his expression, I'm disappointed. Fighting to keep my voice steady, I add, "Unless you've changed your deadline already?"

I sound so confident, so sure of myself. Inside, I'm shaking, replaying the scene in the kitchen over and over again. At any other time, I would have been brought to my knees by the horror of the realization. He was right. All this time, Hale was right, in more ways than he knew. I can't even fathom that the man I grew up with could be capable of such horrific things, but here we are...

Many explanations don't exist for why he could be holding people captive in a crawl space below a country estate. My heart breaks with every passing second. I don't know how I keep standing. Keep from breaking.

But I do.

"You will be married tonight," he says cryptically, drawing my attention to yet another obstacle in the way of my freedom. I'm not sure why, but his tone makes my heart race. It was almost as if he was mocking these impending nuptials. What the hell happened between the last time we spoke and now? Something terrifying. Looking at him more closely, I am alarmed by the changes I detect.

I don't think he's slept for days. In their too-large eye sockets are two lifeless dark irises devoid of light. His wrinkled suit hangs on him, a stark contrast to his usually polished appearance. With pale skin stretched taunt over hollow bones, he appears skeletal from this angle, bathed in the light filtering in through lacey curtains. I can't even explain in words what seeing him like this does to me. Once upon a time, I believed the devil was the only being in existence who could ever look so haggard.

"You will be married tonight," he says harshly, "but your freedom will begin after. Once you are stripped of your shackles and your need for earthly flesh. I see that now. Only purity can save you."

I wince in grim anticipation. I've never heard him talk like this. As if I were made of glass, he peers right through me with every word he says.

"When I'm married to Colton, I'll belong to him," I counter, raising my voice to match his booming cadence. "That's what he told me. A wife belongs to her husband—"

"You are my flesh, and you will never belong to another," he snarls over me. "Not in your current state while you are corrupted and possessed with evil. The imposter festering inside you must be driven out. I'll see to that."

"Do you think Colton will let you? I won't answer to you after tonight. I'll answer only to him. It's what you taught me, after all. A good wife should be obedient."

If I had insulted him like that a few days ago, I'm sure he would have slapped me. The fact that he does nothing, but smile terrifies me more than any violence I've experienced since this nightmare began. In his anger, he reacts out of rage and impulse.

This is something different. From my experience, he's too calm, and that only signals danger.

"You won't be his wife for very long," he says with a knowing glance that snakes up and down the length of my body. "You were mine first, Abagail. Don't think I'd let you go so easily."

Abagail. The hairs on the back of my neck stand upright. Again, his use of my mother's name seems ominous. The way he said it... There was no detached arrogance in his voice, the way he normally spoke of her. No, this seemed more personal. As if...

As if he thinks I really *am* her.

"Father," I say, softening my tone. "What are you saying? Are you calling off my marriage to Colton?"

Before I can feel hope, he shakes his head, raising an eyebrow. "Oh no, you demon," he hisses, jabbing a spindly finger in my direction. "Your twisted scheme can only be circumvented through this sham. You'll get to watch it unravel from your cursed grave. And I will be here to drive you out of the soul of this child that you have corrupted."

"What are you saying?" I rasp. "It's me. It's me, Frey. I'm not Abagail!"

"We shall see," he says with that chilling half-smile. "Enjoy walking in your stolen skin. I wonder what you will look like once it's all peeled away, and your ruse has finally been exposed..."

My blood runs cold. Since this nightmare began, I've only felt anger and hatred toward my father. Rage for what he did to Hale. Confusion and pain for his supposed role in my mother's death. Maybe in the beginning, I even felt guilty for lying to him. Until that point, I never had before.

The only thing I feel now is a sick sense of dread. It's too late to turn back now. Despite my best efforts, my father will not wake up and see the error of his ways. I don't know a way for us to ever reconcile. Not only have I lost Hale, but I've lost the last remnants of the only family I've ever known.

There is no denying the obvious truth—if I stay here, I won't survive long enough for Daze to save me.

"Catherine," my father commands. In the blink of an eye, she appears at the mouth of the doorway. "Show her to her room. Prepare her. Now."

"Yes, Michael." Taking my hand, she gently leads me up a winding staircase and down a long hallway. When we enter a room near the very end, I remember the razor blade in my grasp. I should hide it, but a part of me is too dazed to even care. I can't get my father's face out of my head. The look in his eye...

It was as if I was already dead.

"What do you think?" Catherine asks nervously. She crosses the room to a massive bed draped in white sheets. I swallow hard at the sight of its stern, wooden headboard, and unforgiving frame. Even Daze's shitty mattress-on-the-floor setup held more appeal. There is no way I could even sleep here, let alone endure Colton's touch.

"Frances?"

I blink to awareness and realize that Catherine's been speaking to me all this time. "What do you think of it?" she asks, nodding downward.

As if on cue, I finally spot the dress lying in wait for me on the bed, and my heart sinks. This is not the white dress I had in mind when the thought of marrying Colton didn't disgust me only weeks ago. In my wildest dreams, I imagined myself wearing a beautiful ivory dress.

As if to mock those expectations, the gown I find sprawling before me is, every single inch, composed of black.

"Your father insisted on the color," Catherine explains. Her hands tremble as she fingers the ebony skirt with a smile that never reaches her eyes. "I know it's probably not what you had in mind, but you're so beautiful, anything you wear will look just stunning. Should we clean you up first?"

She ushers me into a bathroom and runs the water while I stare at the bruised, swollen shadow of myself I find in the mirror. This girl isn't the sweet, naïve Frey that Daze rescued from the rail of a bridge. My father was right. I'm a new creature entirely.

And only God knows what I'm capable of.

Without taking my eyes off this strange new Frey, I finally open my fist to reveal the bloodied razor blade. In lieu of an engagement ring to mark this occasion, it feels like the next best thing.

A promise of what is to come.

ELEVEN

DAZE

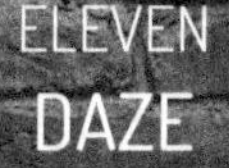

EVEN THOUGH I'M not familiar with his work, it doesn't take long to see why Damien counts Lex as a valued part of the crew. The man is smart as hell. He has spent the past ten minutes explaining, in excruciating detail, how he convinced the reporter to come to this rundown cafe on the outskirts of Westpoint and why.

"Come again?" I ask, forcing Lex to reiterate his plan for the millionth time. The man's whip-thin body resembles a twig next to me, but I know that he is more than capable of handling himself, given the muscles shaping the pale arms bared by his black T-shirt.

"It's simple, really," he says, propping his fist beneath his chin. "I used a method of data scraping and scouring his social media to form a profile of this guy that I could extrapolate to figure out his real intentions."

Gritting my teeth, I say, "In English, that means…"

"His name is Jamie Colland, and he's some up-and-coming hotshot. He's real big on the investigative expose scene, you see?" He takes a sip of coffee from a chipped mug, not that he needs the added caffeine. The man practically vibrates, radiating his own constant supply of energy. In a fight, I'm guessing that comes in handy. "He's all about taking down mainly blue-collar crime, which is what drew his notice to the Heywoods in the first place. Something has him spooked, though. He's been hard to lure out—"

"I know *that*," I snap, fighting to keep my irritation in check. I'm all for respecting other methods of attack—as a fighter, the first thing I learned was that brute strength isn't always the answer. The key to any victory is to outthink and outsmart your opponent.

But right now, I'd rather be beating the shit out of Silas than waiting for some scrawny writer to show his face.

"Tell me something I don't know," I add, watching Lex's eyes sparkle at the challenge.

"Bet. It seems like this guy was intrigued by a bunch of real-estate developments," he says, spreading out his long fingers against the table. "At first. Then a rash of convenient over-doses caught his eye, but do you want to know the real kicker behind what he might have stumbled upon?"

Fuck. I don't like the sound of that. "What?"

"Well—" Lex breaks off and nods to something behind me. "Looks like he showed. You can ask him yourself."

I crane my neck to spy a thin figure slinking toward our section of the café. Despite the fading sunlight, he's wearing a black hoodie with the hood pulled low and a pair of sunglasses. Paired with the black laptop bag slung over his shoulder, it's a wonder someone doesn't mistake him for a suicide bomber and call the fucking police.

"I think you overdid it on the stealth, Nancy Drew," I call out.

He lifts his head enough for me to make out a surprisingly young face with a delicate bone structure. "And you underdid it," he hisses, squeezing into the seat across from me. "Do you not realize that you're one of the most wanted men in the fucking city right now?"

I shrug and point to the baseball cap perched on my head. "This is my idea of stealth."

It doesn't seem important to add that Ben's the one who insisted I add that piece of gear to my ensemble—I was too busy making sure that I didn't wander into the city without being armed to the teeth. Thanks to Damien's connections, I feel more than secure, no matter who might show up to crash this little party.

"I see you didn't exactly come alone," Jamie grouses next, eying Lex, who lurks over my shoulder.

"Tough shit," I counter. "You took the bait, which means you want what I have to share. Now, you tell me what Frey told you."

"By Frey, you mean Frances Heywood," he says. Gingerly, he sets his computer bag on the table between us and takes off his sunglasses. With his wide brown eyes on display, he seems even more like some scrawny punk, nowhere near formidable enough to prove a threat to Heywood and his burgeoning criminal empire. Or, so one might think, if they weren't as familiar with cage fighters as I am. While I doubt he's thrown a punch in his life, this man's stare isn't fearful in the slightest. From the stern tilt to his jaw, he has already sized me up and decided whether he can trust me. For now, he seems cautious.

Smart man.

"She didn't tell me much," he admits. "We were merely able to put the pieces together as to what a certain construction company may be up to. Higher Limit. They've been buying up property here and here—" From his bag, he withdraws a folded piece of paper that he unfurls to reveal a map. One by one, he points to several locations. "These ring a bell?"

"No," I say. "What does this have to do with Michael Heywood?"

Jamie furrows his brows and shrugs. "I think the real question is, what could Michael Heywood accomplish with these properties? It must be something big, because ever since I started making a few phone calls to inquire for a story, I've noticed that I'm being followed. Someone doesn't want these purchases scrutinized."

"He's hiding something," I surmise, cracking my knuckles at the prospect.

"Or, he's storing something," Lex says. "It has all the hallmarks of a smuggling operation."

Jamie nods. "Yes. I figured that as well, but what? And for what purpose?"

"If I had to guess, I'd say terrorist attack."

The reporter raises an eyebrow. "That's quite the leap in judgment to make considering Heywood's background."

"I've seen it before," Lex explains with a slight smile. "I used to do mercenary work for...let's call them 'unorthodox' governments. You wouldn't believe the shit some of those so-called elected leaders would plan just to keep power. Tragedies scare the shit out of people and keep them docile, more willing to sit back idly as their rights get stripped away. Fear is the best fucking motivator of all. So yeah, if Heywood was planning on blowing up half the city, I could buy it."

Jamie sucks his teeth, skeptical. "That sounds like it violates at least several international statutes regarding human rights."

"Probably does," Lex admits. "But the shit still happens every fucking day."

"What kind of attack could Heywood be planning?" I ask, unsure of what to believe. Eyeing the map, I can't make sense of why he'd want to strike those particular locations anyway. They cut through the downtown of the city, but mainly near the docks, coincidentally avoiding a swath of Saints' territory. Though hell, it would make sense for Silas to be on board, if it meant taking out most of his competition in one fell swoop. Still...

"I don't see the point," I say out loud.

"From my vantage point, his aim is something easily contained," Lex remarks, tracing an invisible path that links all the potential locations together. The result is a grim semi-circle with city hall surrounded like an untouched bullseye.

"Like an explosion?" Jamie suggests. "Don't fucking tell me you were on to something..."

"Like the one that destroyed their so-called church building," I say, remembering how freaked Frey had been that day, fearing that her family had been injured. "It could have been a practice run for something bigger."

"Well, if you mark up all those places on the map, what do you see? Is there anything in particular they surround?"

The reporter withdraws a pen and starts marking the locations with an X. Then he draws a circle around the area they all coincidentally encompass.

"Well, I'll be fucked," Lex says with a grin.

I don't share his enthusiasm. Fist clenched, I punch the table hard enough to draw the gaze of a frightened waitress from across the room. "Motherfucker. He's going to wreck half of the city.

And not just any half. Where Lyra lives with Sam. Where my old man's gym is. Most of the Saints' territory and even the church buildings.

"This isn't just chaos he's planning," I say. "It's fucking carnage. He'd destroy his own people if this is the plan."

"What better way to foster sympathy," the reporter points out, an eyebrow raised. "And all but guarantee a victory in the election. Not to mention if there is any evidence of his crimes to be found in the Salvation building or otherwise, well, it'll go up in smoke along with everything else."

"So how do we stop it?" I ask.

The reporter shrugs. "My forte is writing, remember? Besides, this is just a hunch. I can't do anything with speculation and rumors. My editor would laugh me out of his office if I came to him with a doodle. Then he'd send me to the unemployment line. I need some real proof I can take to him. Where is Frances? I'm sure she might have better insight..." He trails off, his eyes on my face. "I'm guessing that's not an option?"

"There isn't time," I mutter, my throat tight. "So, then we cut out the middleman. How do we stop it?"

Lex strokes his chin. "I have some contacts I can call in. Explosives experts. Most of them are out of the country, but I'll see if anyone is close enough to come by now. If we can narrow down where they have the initial charge planned to go off and when, we can sabotage it. The only question is, how do we find that out?"

I have a pretty good fucking idea.

"Heywood couldn't plan something like this on his own. Not the logistics and I doubt he has access to the contacts required to make something like this happen. He's left the planning up to a pasty. A fall guy."

"I see what you're thinking," Lex says. "That's what I would do. So, who do you think?"

I don't have to guess. "Silas. We find him, and he can tell us what we need to know."

The sick son of a bitch has a lot to answer for.

Suddenly, Lex reaches into his pocket, withdrawing a cell phone. Within seconds, his seemingly-permanent grin falls flat. "What is it? Sure, he's right here—" He hands the phone to me. "It's Damien."

Fuck. I doubt he'd be calling now if it wasn't important. "What?" I ask the second I bring the device to my ear.

"Day, I don't want you to panic or anything, but... You might want to get here. Now."

"What the fuck is going on? Is it Frey?"

"It could be," he says, cutting to the chase. "They moved her from the church—"

"What? Why the fuck didn't you tell me?"

"I had Kane tail them just to keep an eye on her. They took her to some fucking mansion outside the city. It's two hours away."

"Fuck. At least you know where she is," I say, but then it strikes me that Damien wouldn't call merely to tell me that. "What else?"

"Kane spotted not just Heywood, but several other cars headed in that direction. They seem to be planning something tonight."

Like a fucking wedding.

My entire body goes numb before I lurch upright. I should have never let them go without me. I should be there with her, not here playing spot the difference.

"I'm going—"

"I'll drive you," Lex says, scrambling to his feet after me. He didn't even hear the full conversation but he's ready to go. "You're coming with," he tells the reporter.

"It's not like I had any plans tonight, anyway," the man says shakily. "Besides, I'm pretty sure we're about to be ambushed. I take it those guys aren't friends of yours?" His gaze is on the window showing a view of the street. At least six men are marching toward the café. The patch on their black vests gives them away without an introduction—Saints.

"Silas always did have perfect fucking timing," I hiss, curling my hands into fists. Sensing movement near my side, I look at Lex. "You ready?"

"Always," he says. Without breaking a sweat, he pulls a pistol from his jacket and aims it toward the doorway. Panicked, the waitress and the only other patrons in the café scream and duck beneath their tables. Unbothered, Lex flashes a grin in my direction. "You?"

"You bet your ass I am."

No one's going to stand in between me and Frey.

No one.

"On the count of three," Lex says. "You cover me, and I'll get us clear."

The reporter scrambles back, clutching his computer bag to his chest. "I guess I'll just stand back here and try not to get shot."

"Deal," I tell him. "Two." Like Lex, I withdraw my weapon and finger the trigger.

"Three," Lex says.

And all hell breaks loose.

Lex fires three warning shots through the front window of the café, shattering the glass and sending a panic through the nearby witnesses. Then he darts toward the back of the café, dragging the reporter by the cuff of his sleeve.

I step back, keeping my eyes on the advancing Saints. They've ducked behind a row of parked cars, but they haven't opened fire. Yet.

That's the worrying part. I'm not the one they give a damn about keeping intact, either. As one of the men pokes his head from around his cover, he spies me and aims.

I barely have enough time to lunge out of his range, in the direction of Lex. The close call proves one very important factor—they're not here for me. The reporter is their target.

And they want him alive.

"Daze, let's go," Lex calls out, and I follow his voice through a side door and out into an alley behind the café, on the opposite end of the street.

There isn't time to parse over what the hell just happened. But even as my ears still ring from the gunfire, I'm smiling as we take off on foot.

For once, I feel like I have not one but two aces up my sleeve.

Two things in my grasp that Silas wants for whatever reason.

If only I knew what the hell that reason actually was.

HOURS LATER, when Catherine finally leads me to a mirror, I bite my lip to keep from making a sound. Ignoring my discomfort, she gently rearranges the veil around my face, revealing the hollow panes of my throat, exposed by a gaping neckline.

"You look so beautiful," she coos. "Oh, Frances, you are stunning!"

In a sense, she's right. I look like a beautiful doll that's been drug through hell and back. Her hair is dull and lifeless despite someone's best attempts to coil it into a lovely bun at the nape of my neck. My makeup is minimal but doesn't do much to add color to my sallow cheeks, and nothing can fully hide the bruises on my face or my swollen bottom lip.

My only comfort is the tiny strip of metal hidden within the hem of one of the long bell sleeves that swallow my arms, leaving my neck and chest as the only sections of bare skin.

Catherine does her best to fuss over me with a plastered smile, but I'm sure we both know the truth. I look like a lamb too battered to slaughter.

"I know the color is a bit unorthodox, but you make it work. You look a picture."

"Do I?" I barely recognize my voice. Although the lips in the mirror move, I feel completely disconnected from the figure gazing back at me with her cold, dead eyes. She is the Frances who attempted to jump into another universe without Daze there to save her.

She lost herself in her grief, fell into the cold bay waters, and this is what was spat back out—a dead woman walking.

"I should go get dressed as well," Catherine mutters, glancing at her wristwatch. "The others will be arriving soon."

"Who?" I ask without tearing my gaze from my reflection. "Who else is coming?"

That is a new detail to this horrific arrangement—spectators. Which of my father's deranged associates might be there? Silas?

"I'm not sure, but Colton is here, and I think he wanted to meet with you," Catherine remarks softly. I can see the pain in her face and hear it in her voice. She may pretend to be oblivious, but even she can't ignore the ominous darkness that looms over this entire house. Something bad is going to happen. I can feel it in the air. I can taste it. The knot of dread and anxiety in my stomach tightens with each passing minute.

Despite my last words, I can't ignore the part of me that wishes Daze would appear on the horizon. However, I know he wouldn't carry me to safety without craving revenge if he saw my face now. He would burn this entire house down with his enemies still inside it.

Would that be such a bad thing?

There is no clear answer anymore. I just want to get out of here as soon as possible—but it's a minor priority. Firstly, I need to rescue those people in the basement and, if possible, find out why they're being held here at all. I can't get the knowledge of their presence out of my head, or the smell. Despite wearing a priceless gown, I feel so helpless while they cower in squalor below.

But nothing compares to the fear I feel at what could be in store for them.

And for me.

When Catherine leaves the room, I pace the narrow space alone. On my tenth pass near the door, I halfheartedly test the lock, unsurprised to find it secured. Even with my sliver of razor blade, I feel exposed. Weak.

Or so the old Frances would be.

Daze taught me well and I scan the room with a renewed focus, finding anything I can use to aid in my escape. There's a lamp on a nightstand in the corner. I unplug it and set it aside within easy reach—if push comes to shove, I can always use it as a weapon. Only then do I feel somewhat more secure.

Now, to gain a greater understanding of what could be taking place beyond this cage. I don't hear footsteps or a guard approaching after pressing my ear to the door. From below, a distant commotion can be heard near the house's front. Faint voices. Murmurs of conversation. My pulse begins to race as an unfamiliar baritone rumbles in the air. Could this be the arrival of those mysterious "others" that Catherine hinted at?

As I imagine what sort of people could associate with my father, I shudder. No one good.

Trying to make out any noise from below, I sink to my knees, desperate for more. Gradually, the sounds shift, forcing me to inch from the door to a distant corner of the room. Within seconds, I'm crouched near a vent in the floor at the back of the room, straining to pick up traces of that initial conversation. I can almost make out my father's voice, but all I hear are...

Whimpers. There are three distinct voices, so soft I can barely hear them. They don't seem to convey a sense of danger that would justify Catherine's reluctance, though. Not my father's cohorts, perhaps. In fact, I can still hear him, but his voice comes from the other direction of the house.

"Shhh," I hear one of the figures seemingly below the vent whisper. Her voice is so clear that it seems like she's in the room next to me. "They're coming."

I strain my ears for any approaching footsteps, but none reach this level, meaning...

Could I be hearing the people in the basement?

It feels like an unlikely scenario at first—but then I remember our old house and how Hale and I used to pretend to be ghosts, whispering messages to each other using the vents. From the bottom level in the sunroom, he could hear me all the way in his room, a story above.

After a tense few moments of silence, a heavy sigh of relief echoes, followed by terse shushing. Tentatively, I decide to call out, "Hello?"

Silence greets me in return. I can't even hear so much as an intake of air. My cheeks flame. Already, I've gone insane, forced to speak to the shadows if only to distract from the state my life is currently in. Then I hear a set of footsteps approaching from the hall, too suddenly to have come from the stairs.

Shit!

As I begin to rise, a faint sound reaches my ears. "Is someone there?"

In the blink of an eye, the doorknob turns, and I'm still on my knees when the door itself swings open to reveal a smirking Colton.

In contrast to my black gown, he's dressed in a pure-white tux. How cliché. I'm sure he and my father snickered over the juxtaposition—his innocent visage paired with mine, woefully corrupted.

Ironically, even as haggard as I appear, I think Colton looks worse, like a fanciful caricature of his former self. Or, what an innocent fool might imagine a nice, wholesome man to be. Almost like he's playing dress up with someone else's clothes.

There will never be a day when I won't marvel at how easily he and my father fall into their new roles as villains. My entire life has been filtered through rose-colored glasses. As I sleepwalked through my past life, what else had I missed?

After looking me up and down with narrowed eyes, Colton declares, "You look God awful, Frances. I thought Catherine might be able to do something with your face. Apparently not."

His disapproval means nothing to me. Still, I can't stop myself from self-consciously brushing a hand along my cheek. As soon as I realize, I stop myself and keep my head held high. I am not ashamed of the bruises and injuries I've acquired over the past few weeks. Scars and all, they should be worn as badges of honor.

I can't ignore the little voice in my head that wonders what Daze will think of me, though. *If* I ever see him again...

"I thought I should meet with you before the ceremony just in case you had any delusions of grandeur. Tonight, your father no longer holds any dominion over you, Frances Heywood. You will belong to me. Body and soul."

I dislike the way he uttered the last three words. As his eyes rake over me with way too much familiarity, I step back. My hand flies to the cuff of my sleeve, hunting the razor blade hidden there, just beneath the satin and lace. I don't withdraw it. Yet.

"Oh, don't pretend to be coy, Frances," Colton snarls, stepping forward. "I'm sure you gave more than a glimpse of your body to that biker motherfucker. Didn't you?" He grabs my wrist, jerking me forward.

Panic darts through my system, but I fight to keep my head clear, even as his breath fans over my face. *Don't panic. Breathe, Frey. You can handle this.*

But if I pull it out now, there goes my entire leverage. Until I'm certain I can escape, I need to stall.

"You never brought me here," I say, hoping to distract him. "Where are we exactly? Is this one of your family's properties—"

"Don't!" Without warning, he reaches out and grabs my throat. Though my eyes bulge, I don't resist. I'm already trying to work the razor blade free when he loosens his hold.

"Don't think you can play sweet and coy with me, Frances," he growls, his teeth bared. "Not after the humiliation you put me through. I loved you once. I thought you to be a worthy woman to marry. I used to imagine the sort of children we would have, hopefully with your beautiful eyes. But now I see that any children born of you will be as corrupted with evil as you are. If they aren't purified first. Only the hand of a stern father can prevent such a devious nature from festering and spreading. But don't worry, Frances—" He grabs my chin and yanks my face within inches of his. "I fully intend to make sure that you embody the good, God-fearing woman you used to be. And more. You will grow to love me, I'm sure of it. And I fully intend to take advantage of your wifely duties..." I see his arm move and tense even before I feel him touching me—his other hand bunches handfuls of my skirt, lifting it...

Thinking fast, I entwine our fingers together, pulling his hand away.

"If you loved me, you would have told me the truth from the start," I say, trying and failing to make my voice a simpering mockery of how I used to sound. Weak. Passive. He draws his eyebrows together, his skepticism evident, but to my surprise, he relaxes into my grasp. "I only turned to someone else because I felt alone. I was so lost in grief after Hale. It seemed like no one else cared."

He stares into my eyes for a long moment. Then he squeezes my hand so hard I gasp.

"It was your duty to be patient," he warns. "Said attribute is a virtue, after all. You should have been silent by my side and trusted that your father and I knew best. That it would all be for the greater good. You shouldn't have given yourself away to some miscreant like a harlot at the first sign of doubt! And if you truly knew what your father and I had in store, there is no telling what you might do..."

"I would have trusted you," I lie. As if the words physically hurt, the inside of my cheek smarts, and every bruise I sport begins to ache tenfold. "I would have known that you were being honest with me. That's also a virtue."

He tenses his shoulder again, and I'm certain he'll hit me. The fact that he doesn't move brings little comfort. The look in his eye promises only malice. Retribution.

"You think you're so damn smart. Fine. Then why don't you tell me what that degenerate you fucked had to say. Or did you even get as far as talking before you offered yourself to him on a silver platter?"

I fight to keep my anger at bay. He wants me riled and liable to slip up. I refuse to give him the satisfaction.

"He told me that Hale didn't kill himself," I say, watching his reaction carefully. "He told me that I couldn't trust anyone."

"Like me?" He pulls back, his eyes narrowing. "And I'm sure you believed him. Dear God, Frances. You always were gullible, but even that should have aroused the smallest hint of skepticism from you."

He sounds so damn cocky. Too smug to be lying. It suddenly occurs to me that he doesn't know the full truth. Apparently, my father doesn't trust him as much as he does Silas. It brings something else he said into a new, chilling light. He may be forcing me to marry Colton, but he doesn't intend for me to stay married long.

Why is that?

"I thought Father trusted you," I say, choosing to probe Colton outright. "Perhaps I should speak more to the man he had keep me company the other night."

"Don't be stupid." Colton scoffs, but I can see confusion ripple across his expression. Apparently, he was still sour about Silas' visit, and the thought unnerves me. Clearly, Colton's role in this twisted game has an end date, one my father even alluded to. Tonight?

"Look at me, you little cunt—" He rips his hand from mine, forcing me to face him. "What the hell are you talking about?"

"What?" I try to keep my face blank, knowing the lack of fear will further enrage him. "You mean he didn't tell you? That he sent another man to keep me company *all night*. Some husband you are. Doesn't the Bible say that a man should guard his woman above all else?"

"You little..." He pulls his arm back, curling his hand into a fist—but then he stops. A flit of hesitation crosses his face as if he just remembered something crucial. Perhaps a warning uttered to him by Father in terms that he can't ignore? He can't touch me. Not tonight. There is a show to put on, after all, and it seems my father wants us both to look and play the part.

"It seems that you're constantly taking orders when it comes to me," I say, laughing as his cheeks redden. "Even now, you know that you will never be able to control me. Not one damn bit. You are nothing more than my father's puppet."

"Is that so?" His hand collides with my shoulder, spinning me around. As I sway to find my balance, pain sears through my scalp, and a glance in the nearby mirror reveals why—he ripped off my veil, pulling my hair out of its delicate coil. I can feel loose strands fall down my shoulders as tears prick my eyes. It hurts like hell, but I'd rather die than show it.

"You smart-mouthed little cunt," he says, his voice rising. "You think he has you so protected? You have no idea how hard I had to fight for him to even keep you in the city and let you marry me. His original plans for you, Frances, were far more befitting. Thankfully, he realized that the money you could bring would make you more useful to keep alive, but don't think that I can't change his mind. All I have to do is walk away."

"Then why don't you?" I counter, turning to face him directly. "I'm sure he would love to give me to Silas. A man he actually trusts—"

I hear the slap more than I really feel it. My vision goes black for a heartbeat, before returning in snatches. Brilliant stars still dance before my eyes as Colton reappears before me, adjusting his tie.

"You made me do that," he grumbles, eyeing me with a look of utter disgust. "I'm sure your father will understand. From what I hear, your mother was a feisty one as well."

Don't, a part of me warns as anger washes over me. *Don't take the bait. Don't let him rattle you.*

Too late. As fresh blood drips from the reopened wound on my inner cheek, restraint seems damn near impossible to maintain. My situation resembles that of an animal trapped in a cage, about to be forced to decide between fighting to escape or submitting to death. It's becoming clearer to me now more than ever. I won't last the night here.

So, I decide to throw tact to the wind.

"Don't worry, Colton." Red liquid sprays as I speak, no doubt splattering over my exposed neckline. "I'm sure if you find me too feisty for you, you can help yourself to one of the poor women you have locked up on the property. My father told me all about them as well."

For a split second, his face flashes with genuine concern. Panic takes root in my chest as I realize one chilling detail—I've caught him off guard. Could he not know?

"I'm sure you have no idea," I rush to add. "Some important partner you are. You're nothing more than a puppet dangling from a pretty string—"

"Shut up!" Lightning fast, he slaps me again, but I manage to deflect the blow with the back of my hand. I feel riled. My skin heats as though a live wire is thrumming beneath it, prickling hot, ready to burn anything or anyone who dares to get too close. An unpleasant metallic taste is on my tongue, but it's not blood. It's anger. I wonder if this is what Daze feels in those moments of blackout rage. When he seemed like a creature possessed more than a man.

Do I have the same look in my eye? For some reason, the prospect doesn't terrify me. I *want* to be like him.

"You deluded yourself, Colton," I spit, laughing at his shocked expression. "You think that you matter, but you're as disposable as I am. He told me so. You claimed you'd have dominion over me after the wedding. Do you want to know what my father said when I told him?" I force another cold laugh from my throat that sounds gleeful. Demonic. "He said that it won't last very long. That you will never outrank him when it comes to me. Why do you think that is?"

"And did your father tell you that *he'll* be lucky if he even survives tonight?" he asks in a hoarse hiss. "You think you know everything, you smug little bitch. Then you riddle me this—who needs your father if they can control access to your mother's estate? Michael Heywood is a fading star. Do you know who could benefit politically from his demise, however? His grieving son-in-law. Don't make the mistake of assuming that your father is the only one with ambitions, Frances."

He shoves me back so hard I land on the bed, breathless. He steps forward to loom over me, cracking his knuckles one by one.

"I was going to wait until our wedding night to teach you the importance of obedience when it comes to your husband," he says, his voice low and menacing. "But I think I'll make an exception. After all, you're already mine whether you want to believe it or not. Once I get your signature on the marriage certificate, you or your father won't have any legal recourse. So why should I wait to see what my own wife has to offer?"

He snatches a handful of my skirt and wrenches it up. Cold air teases my skin before his groping fingers replace it, scratching and clawing. My mind goes blank, but not out of panic. A steely finality comes over me. *This is it*, it warns. *You won't get another chance. Hurting him won't be enough this time. You need to kill...*

The silk of my dress feels like sandpaper beneath my searching fingertips as they hunt for a hint of sharpness tucked within the lace. There. If I aim for Colton's throat, it doesn't matter how tiny my blade is—as long as I hit an artery. Swallowing hard, I start to wind the metal loose as Colton lunges toward me, raising his hand...

A knock rattles the door, attracting his attention just paces from me. "What is it?"

An unfamiliar voice replies. "Sir, everyone is meeting in the stables for the ceremony."

Colton eyes his raised fist and laughs as if he finds the violence amusing. Gradually, he resumes his polished persona, straightening his tie once again. Tilting his head toward the door, he says, "We'll be down in a moment."

The expression on his face isn't what I expect a new husband to show to his wife. Icy, his narrowed gaze promises painful retribution next time we're alone.

"Compose yourself," he snaps while marching toward the door. I make a halfhearted attempt to tie back my hair, not that he seems to care. After smoothing a hand down the front of his suit, he pulls the door open to reveal a guard, nearly identical to the others I'd glimpsed skulking around the property. Dressed in black with a weapon at his hip, he waits patiently for Colton and me to exit the room. As we head toward the staircase, the guard follows, his steps echoing like a morbid countdown.

Tick.

Tock.

This is another glaring sign that, despite Colton's pompous demeanor, he's not as in control as he thinks. Taking in everything I can, I push the fear aside as we pass the same rooms adorned with faded luxury that I saw while with Catherine. After the sun sets behind the tall windows, the darkness doesn't provide a better contrast to this place than the bright daylight did. In disrepair and dust, it appears more like a gothic vampire's lair.

Or a prison.

A sense of déjà vu washes over me as we retreat down a vaguely familiar corridor that ends before a set of ornate black doors. Another guard opens them from the outside, revealing a shadowed courtyard enclosed by seemingly endless swaths of forest. Colton nudges me out before him as I strain my eyes to view a neglected lawn with overgrown hedges. Not far from the house is an empty fountain that's been dry long enough for weeds to have grown up between cracks in the stone base. Looming above it, towering in the darkness, is a set of large, triangular buildings that must be the stables. Orange lanterns have been fixed to the outside of one, illuminating two large doors left open to the night air.

Apprehension floods my veins. It's not the church venue I was expecting. The uneasy sensation of stage fright envelops me as hushed murmurs from within the imposing structure seep out to greet me. I feel as if I am the lead in a twisted production I never agreed to participate in.

I look over at Colton, whose eyes gleam with a smug air of superiority. As we approach the stables, he grasps my hand in a punishing grip, but I know better than to pull away.

Even though I cannot see him, I can feel my father watching me from the faceless crowd before us. God, there must be twenty... thirty people here. Can any of them be from the congregation in which I spent my entire life, now corrupted by the evil of my father? Only a torchlight illuminates the mostly-dark interior, causing my eyes to blink rapidly as Colton drags me inside.

I glance up at the "altar" ahead, and my heart sinks deeper into my chest. When I used to consider marriage, I envisioned a grand, beautiful ceremony, with my father there to guide me down the aisle and a crowd of swooning church-goers dressed in their Sunday best.

I don't recognize any of the shrouded figures assembled here. They seem formless, as if draped in black cloaks that shield their features from view. Faceless onlookers, they stand gathered around the sides of the stables, watching in an eerie coordinated silence as Colton and I traverse a long walkway lined in black carpet.

I don't like this.

Especially when I finally see what lurks beyond the altar, emanating a sweltering heat. I don't know how I missed it before—a stone basin containing a roaring fire that crackles at the air. A man in a black robe stands beside it, a hood drawn low over his face.

I can't help it. I falter, forcing Colton to tug on my wrist sternly.

"Come on," he hisses. "I swear I'll drag you there if I have to."

He might have to. What the hell is going on? I can't see my father anywhere. At least until the hooded figure speaks, his voice low and gravelly but instantly familiar.

"Come forward, both of you, and allow yourself to be honored by the cleansing fire."

Fire. My eyes widen at the word. Despite their terrible beauty, I can't help but stare at the dancing flames. I must stop short a second time, because Colton nearly pulls me to the floor in his irritation to force me to keep up.

For a heartbeat, all the bravery I've amassed over the past few days goes out the window. I can't breathe. Terror forms a stone ball in the pit of my throat, making it impossible to suck in air. My heart is a quivering mass in my chest, and my knees buckle.

Cleansing fire.

Cleansing fire.

Those two words form a ceaseless mantra that taunts me, drowning out any voice of reason in my mind that might argue with it. I can't go through with this. *I can't!*

My fingers are ready to pry the razor blade free.

Then I see them.

Initially, their location appears obscured from my vantage point. In this winding, echoing chamber, I can only hear their hushed whimpers, soft and fearful. My ears are captivated by the sound, and I turn my head just enough to make out shadows in a nearby stall. The place seems devoid of horses, but instead, there are three small figures huddled together on a heap of hay. Loose, dark hair tumbles down their shoulders and every one of them would make a more fitting bride than I do. They're dressed in white shifts that expose their knees and hang on their slender frames as if no one bothered to size them properly.

Because they won't be wearing them for very long, a voice in my head explains. *You remember what Father said. That word—Sacrifice.*

I shake my head, desperate to clear it of the paranoid whispers. Before I know it, Colton and I are standing before the hooded figure, facing the burning pyre.

This close, it's easier to tell that the ebony-clad figure is my father. Or at least he used to be. As he throws back his hood, I can't find any shred of Michael Heywood lurking within those empty eyes. Gone is any ounce of warmth or light. His very soul seems to reflect the darkness in this room, making even the fire reflecting off his irises seem cold and lifeless.

"We are here today to recognize the holy union of these two souls," he says, his voice overly loud, echoing off the walls in an endless din. "May they both be joined in eternal bonds, but to strengthen those bonds, a promise must be made, and a promise must be kept..."

A cry goes up from the back of the room. The guard who followed us in stands apart from the crowd, herding all three girls from the stall. They're no older than I am, tethered together by shackles on their ankles, and their wide eyes make them resemble a trio of innocent does, captured purely for some hunter's amusement.

My heart sinks. *This isn't right,* that voice in my head warns. *This isn't right. Run, Frey. Run!*

Colton digs his nails into the back of my hand as if sensing my thoughts. "You think you are any different than they are?" he asks me, his voice dangerously soft. "You're not, and if you so much as try to disobey me, you'll end up the same way. I'll see to it."

I barely hear him. My attention is consumed by the guard as he crouches to free one of the girls from her companions. She staggers forward, resembling a dove fluttering through the crowd of silent, darkened onlookers. They move in unison, herding her toward the stage as she glances around wildly, visibly confused.

I feel a desperate impulse to help her. *Do something. Move.* The second I take a step, Colton wrenches me back.

"Don't," he snaps.

"What are you doing?" My voice echoes wildly. "Tell me!"

"This is a necessary act that you brought upon yourself," my father says, filling the entire room. "You are the reason that this union needs to be purified, because of your lies and evil."

Purified. That word haunts me as the frightened girl is steered to the altar and forced to mount it. I feel her grab my hand as she passes.

"Please help me, please!"

I don't recognize her, but a sickening suspicion tells me that she's most likely from the Salvation outreach program, lured here under false pretenses.

But to what end?

Again, I try to speak. "What's going on?"

"Consider this my wedding present to you," my father continues. "And a reminder. Should you think to do anything to me or to destroy this marriage, this will happen."

He lunges for the girl as two men surge from the crowd to help wrestle her down onto a flat table I'd missed before, positioned directly beneath the pyre. She cries out in alarm as they hold her in place while my father approaches. It is only when he brandishes an object into the air that the shape of what he is holding becomes apparent.

A knife.

"No!"

Colton hooks his arm around my waist from behind, pinning me against him. Trapped, I can only watch in horror as the man I once called Father lowers the blade over the girl's chest.

And plunges it in.

"No!" I lose track of myself. I'm not even aware of biting or hitting or flailing at my captors—only that nothing I do can get me free in time.

Bit by bit, I watch the blood spill onto the floor.

And in those wide, endless brown eyes, I see the life drain out.

I UNDERSTAND TERROR AND AGONY. After all, I've become well acquainted with both emotions these past few days. But rage? Hatred...

I am blinded by those new sensations, and I cannot think rationally. I just see red. The sound of the blood ramming against my eardrums, is all I can hear. The constant thrumming echoes in my head like a chant. Fight. Fight. Kill. Kill.

My rage is followed by numbness that paralyzes me before I can even comprehend it. I'm numb. Frozen. Throughout the wedding ceremony, I submit meekly over a blood-stained altar like a doll. I can hear the smothered cries and fearful pleas of the two surviving girls somewhere behind me.

And I can gaze into the empty, staring eyes of the girl before me, seeing nothing. Like a morbid soundtrack to this nightmare, my father's voice drones on and on.

"...By the rights vested in me, I declare you both bound in holy matrimony, a union that has been purified and blessed.

May you both live long enough to enjoy the fruits of this marriage."

I'm in a daze as Colton finally shepherds me from the stables toward the house. I only snap back to myself when a door slams, and I realize I'm locked in the room with Colton.

"Get on the bed," he commands, stripping his jacket. "Now."

I slap his hand away. "Don't touch me."

He puffs up his chest, his head cocked. "Did you not just see what happened out there? The lengths your father is willing to go through? That was a convincing show. Next time, I'll kill one of those girls for real."

"Real?" I blink, unable to reconcile his statement with reality. I saw the blood. Tasted it. Felt it. There is no way in hell that wasn't real. Unless...

The same way my father has lost his mind, Colton is losing all sense of reality. That fact makes him a more dangerous opponent than I realized.

"That was real, you fucking dumbass," I snap. "Did you not see that with your own eyes? You think that he'll stop at those girls? He'll kill you too! He'll probably kill both of us!"

"Stop being dramatic, Frances." Colton towers over me and slams me down with such force that I am left gasping for breath. "You shouldn't concern yourself with anything but what I expect from you tonight. Your criminal bastard isn't here to save you, and I intend to take advantage of every part of yourself that you gave to him. Starting with this—" I feel him groping me clumsily through the waist of my gown, and instinct takes over.

He grunts when I kick him so hard, he falls backward.

"You stupid little bitch." He looks up from the floor, his eyes wild. "I'll make you pay for that. Real or not, I'll drag you back to that place and cut you with that knife. Or perhaps I'll convince your father to stop playing with your lover. Why should he die in a blaze of glory like the others? I say we capture him tonight and cut out his heart while you watch. Would you like that?" Teeth bared, he lunges for me.

"No!" I kick him again, grappling for leverage. As I hear fabric tear and feel nails gouging my inner thigh, I know I won't be able to fight him off. Not physically.

So, I don't think about the consequences or the concept of right and wrong. Reaching out, I grab the nearest item within reach—the lamp. Gripping it tight, I swing it as hard as I can toward him.

He makes an inhuman sound and staggers off, swiping at his face with his hands.

"Like mother like daughter," he snarls, his teeth bared and streaked with blood. The blow must have split his lip. Menacingly, he reaches for me. "You're going to end up just like her—"

"No!" I throw myself toward him. There's warm blood on my cheek, but I barely even feel it as I peel the razor blade free and throw myself forward, jamming it into any part of him I can reach. His face. His chest.

"You crazy bitch," he grunts out, lashing at me with a closed fist.

"I am," I counter, ignoring the blow that glances off my right eye. "I am a crazy bitch!"

It's all I can say, and over again, as I keep striking him. Over and over, until he finally falls silent, and I can think clearly again.

As the door opens and someone steps inside, I don't care. Somewhere at the back of my mind, I mourn for Daze. I'll never see him again. The crazy, sexy idiot with charming gray eyes will never know just how much I love him.

I'll never taste him again.

At least he won't see me the way I am now, covered in blood, wide-eyed, and crazed. I have a clear view in the mirror across from me, but the person staring back isn't any iteration of Frey I've glimpsed until now. Clothed in black, with her blond hair streaked red, she's a demon.

"Frances..." The voice seems to come from miles away, barely able to penetrate the stupor I'm in. It's like I'm no longer attached to my body, but floating somewhere above, watching on with indifference. While I can see Colton lying on his back, covered in blood, I don't feel anything.

Not panic, not terror, not even guilt.

I feel nothing at all.

"Frances, honey, look at me." Someone is running their fingers through my hair in a smooth, gentle motion. *Not my father,* a part of me realizes, but I don't know who else the figure could be. My vision is limited to what is directly in front of me—Colton. His blood is forming a slowly growing puddle that seeps into the skirt of my dress. The funny thing about black silk is that it obscures any stains that might occur.

Despite the carnage around me, I seem untouched.

"Frances, honey, please! Look at me!" The stroking fingers leave my hair to brush my cheek. "Please. We don't have much time."

As I blink, I finally see the beautiful figure kneeling beside me, her face contorted in horror.

"C-Catherine?"

"Yes, it's me." I feel her soft hands pulling me to my feet as she nods. "It's ok, darling. I'm here."

Wait... A cold jolt of panic shoots through me as I look back at Colton. If she's here, my father can't be far behind. The remaining girls will be killed just to punish me. I can't let that happen. I can't. A sharp pain across my palm draws my attention downward—I'm still holding the bloodied razor.

"Frances, look at me!"

Catherine pulls her hand back and strikes my cheek. I feel the pain like a delayed response to a hot stove. Nothing at first, then burning, molten heat all at once.

"Snap out of it and listen to me!" I have never heard Catherine raise her voice before, but now it echoes off the walls. "We don't have much time," she insists, darting her gaze to the closed door. "Michael has left with the others, but Colton was due to check in via telephone soon. I'm sure Michael would have had him killed anyway. But this is your only chance to run, do you hear me? Go now into the woods, and don't look back!" She shrugs off her blue jacket and drapes it over my shoulders, revealing a simple gray dress underneath. I don't remember seeing her at the wedding. Where was she?

Suddenly, English seems nearly impossible to understand. "Run?"

"Yes, run! I'll handle things here. Just run and don't look back!"

As she shoves me to the door, I feel as if I am wading through water. Suddenly, one clear thought penetrates the haze of my mind.

"The girls. There are two other women. I need to find them—"

"Of course!" Catherine nods. "They'll be in the stables, I think. Somewhere close by, but I'm not sure. I can't guarantee their safety. I only care about you. You're right. I failed Hale, but I won't stand aside and do nothing anymore. Whatever you decide, I'll try to buy you time. Just trust me, please."

I don't know whether or not I can. There is a possibility that she and my father are conspiring to ensnare me in an elaborate trap. The paranoia is unbearable, but I manage to snap out of it with a firm shake of my head.

"What about the guards?"

"They're distracted," she says with another frantic look at the door. "For now. I told them Colton demanded privacy. Go out through the back. By the time you make it outside, I'm sure you'll be the last thing on their minds. Just trust me, please, and whatever you do... Know that I always cared about you and Hale. Truly, I did. I do."

Something unspoken lurks within her words. A part of her plan that she intentionally isn't telling me outright. No doubt, something dark and dangerous.

Still, I can't deny the gratitude I feel for her, after everything. Reaching out, I take her hand. "Thank you."

She inhales deeply as her eyes fly to our clasped hands. "I..." Suddenly, she cocks her head as a sound rumbles from below.

"Go!" She shoves me forward. "Go now!"

I scramble into the hall and follow her instructions, surprised to find the winding corridors empty. In her coat, I feel like a ghost, unnoticed by everyone, and yet the slightest noise might give me away. As I make my way outside, I can't help but feel like it was all too easy. It was a trick. A trap. My father will be waiting for me in the courtyard, ready to snuff out another innocent life at my expense.

However, I see nothing but darkness as my vision adjusts, except for a faint orb of light denoting the stables. It only takes me a split second to make up my mind. Rather than escape toward the road, I head toward the set of buildings, unsure of what I'll find.

Suddenly, shouts rise up from the house. Then, the crash of broken glass. Startled, I turn back and stare. On the second story, I recognize the window of the room Colton imprisoned me in. Only now, orange flames lick at the glass, glowing in the darkness.

Catherine. I start to return in the direction I came from, but then I stop mid-step as her plea echoes in my mind. *Trust me.*

With a heavy heart, I turn around and run blindly toward the stables. Despite my attire, two guards run right past me toward the house. In the stables, one remains, peering warily from the entrance, and behind him, I can see the place where the girls were kept, the door closed.

I look around and find a shovel. It's heavy, but I use what strength I have left to heft it as high as I can. When I approach the guard, he doesn't even have time to cry out. I watch his body fall, and a strange panic comes over me when all I feel is nothing.

It's like I'm sleepwalking to the stall, fumbling with the lock.

"The keys," someone cries out to me. "He has the keys."

I turn back to the guard and shove my hands into his pockets. In one, I find a set of keys that gleam in the darkness. On unsteady feet, I race back to the stable and shove one of the keys into the lock. On the third try, I get the door open and discover two frightened figures huddled at the back of the enclosed space.

"We're chained," one of them says, pointing to her ankles.

The key for the door works, and once they're freed, they scurry to the doorway. "We need to go now, because when they come back..." She breaks off abruptly, her gaze fixed on the house. As I follow in their wake, I realize why.

The entire house is on fire, a blazing inferno of orange flames that swallows the top of the structure. Suddenly, Catherine's parting words to me make sense. This is what she meant by not looking back.

"We need to go." I head toward the woods, unsure of where the hell I'm going or how. The guards will only be distracted for a few moments, if that. I can hear the girls in my wake as we stagger near the main road.

Only God knows what will happen next.

DAZE

I'LL NEVER FORGIVE myself for putting her second. While Lex drives like a bat out of hell, that's all I can think about. This sick feeling inside me warns that it's already too late. I failed her.

She's injured, hurt, or dead, and I failed her.

Just to keep the rage at bay, I grind my teeth. Centered. It was easy for me to cut off all emotion before she came along. In the case of Renna, I was able to distance myself from the pain. I cared for her. I lost her. I moved on.

But this...

With every breath, the pain grows sharper. There's nothing I can do but rock in my seat, ready to fight. Kill if I have to.

For once, my thoughts of violence don't numb me like they usually do. In this vicious, never-ending game of *Daze Fucked Up*, they just feed on themselves.

There's no recovering from this mistake.

"How much longer?" I snap.

Taking a hand off the wheel, Lex gestures toward the speedometer. "Soon." His gaze is narrowed, fixed on the road with ruthless focus. If this really is the right location, the road there is mostly deserted—a fact I don't like one damn bit. There should be security everywhere, intensifying the closer we get.

"It should be over that ridge up ahead," Lex says after another few minutes of silence. "Right there... Holy shit."

I see it at the same time he does—fire swallowing what used to be a mansion on some country estate. The lack of patrols suddenly makes perfect sense—they're all fighting the blaze.

And I know, somehow, someway, that Frey is here, trapped in that fucking house.

"Daze, wait!"

My ears barely register Lex's voice as I leap from the van, charging through the woods between the vehicle and the mansion. With a single-minded focus, I propel myself forward. I don't give a damn if I'm a sitting duck or an easy target. I don't give a damn if a thousand of Heywood's thugs swarm me before I can even set foot near that house.

All I care about is getting to her. Finding her. If she's in there...

"Have you lost your fucking mind?" Someone shouts near my ear, panting in their effort to keep up. The voice is familiar, but my brain is too wired to process it. All I know is when they place their hand on my shoulder their aim is to stop me. Keep me from her. "Daze, wait!"

"Get the fuck off me—" I form a fist and let it fly, then I keep gunning for the blaze up ahead. I can make out shapes running in the dark. Guards shouting and coordinating a search effort.

"They're still inside," I swear I hear one of them say. "The door was fucking locked."

No...

"Daze, slow the fuck down!"

More hands grab me from behind. There must be three, four, different pairs of hands clawing at every part of me in an attempt to slow me down. Friend or foe, I don't fucking care. Fighting blindly, I swing like hell.

All I can see is the fire. All I can see is her face the last time I held her. *Trust me*, she said, making it sound so fucking easy. Trust her. Invest the same amount of faith in her as she did in me.

As a result, I may have lost her forever.

"Fuck, Daze! Don't make me taser your ass."

Finally, the identity of one of the voices shouting in my ear hits me—Ben. He's standing in front of me, wiping blood from his chin as three other men try to wrestle me to the ground.

"Are you listening to me? You go in there, and you'll be killed on sight, you idiot. It's a fucking hornets' nest. You want to do this, we got to do this right."

"Right?" I don't even recognize the sound of my voice. I don't show emotion so raw. Not when my old man died. Not with Renna. Never. Then, to chase away the pain, comes a familiar rage that hardens me against any hint of emotion.

Damn, Frey. Damn her. If she left me like this, I'll follow her straight to heaven, even if I have to fight my way out of hell. I won't let her go this easily.

"Daze, for fuck's sake. I know you're worried about her, but you need to listen—"

"Get the fuck off me, Ben. Or so help me God, I won't hold back."

"Listen to yourself," Ben shouts, his tone firm. "Think. You'll just get yourself killed acting like this, or do you really not give a damn about her at all?"

That final jab reaches me, and I go limp. He's right. Not that it fucking matters.

"She's dead," I croak. "You heard them."

"No one's dead until the fat lady sings," Damien says. He's one of the men that releases me, his hands raised. Beside him, I see Marco who takes a step back. "We do this, then we do it right. I know you got your girl in there, but right now, it's a hotbed. You hear that?" He cocks his head, listening.

"I don't hear shit," I say.

"Exactly. No fire sirens. No ambulances. No paramedics. That means they want this mess locked down tight, even if the bastard's daughter could be in that ruin. Why do you think that is?"

He's right. Panting, I look around and take stock of the obvious. It's too quiet. There isn't even a helicopter in the fucking sky to survey the damage. Judging from the smoldering remnants of the house, they've just let the motherfucker burn with no attempts to quash the blaze. I'm angry at the thought, but then I push it aside to see it from the perspective of a detached mercenary.

"They don't want this getting out," I say thickly. The smell of smoke is thick even from here. "Whatever they had here... They don't want it known, not even by the fire department or police."

"Exactly," Ben says, stroking his chin. He moves to crouch beside me and paws at the damp ground before us. "The place went up fast. Definitely arson. Must have been set from the inside."

"God, no..." I keep hearing the guard's words echoing in my head. *The door was fucking locked. The door was fucking locked.* "Fuck, Frey." My knees buckle under me. It feels as if someone kicked me in the chest, then pulled out a pistol to finish the job.

I imagine her trapped in the mangled remains of that house. All because I took so long to play detective. She needed me here. I should have never let her go.

"Day, I'm going to try and get a better vantage point—" Ben ducks beneath the branches of a nearby tree, heading toward the outskirts of the house. "I'll see how many guards there are. If we play this right, we might be able to take them on and get to the house."

"I don't give a shit." I shrug off the grief and let the bitter rage wash over me, giving me the strength to stand. "I'm going in there."

"Well, just give us five minutes, Day," Damien says while scanning the area. "Can you give us that? For now, you take two guys and check the road. We'll clear the house. You'll get to her, no matter where she is, you have my word on that."

Several seconds later, Ben emerges from a thicket of trees, panting. "Come on, Day," he says, nodding toward the manor. "The coast seems clear. Let's see if any of those assholes are waiting in the woods."

I don't need to be told twice.

Following him, I tear through the narrow clearing that surrounds the property's outskirts. This place would have been fancy as hell in its heyday, a place where Frey would have belonged. It's the kind of home I could never give her.

Another crushing wave of guilt makes me grunt at the thought. If she really went up in that blaze...

The only way I can keep moving is to turn my brain off. Tuning into every sound and twitch of tree branches rustling in the wind, I focus on listening. Only a few yards from the road, I hear a noise that makes me curl my fists in anticipation—advancing footsteps. They're soft, aiming for stealth, but nowhere near quiet enough. Some professional fucking guards they are. In lieu of fighting the fire and searching for survivors, they prefer to traipse through the woods.

I speed up, my nostrils flared, as I try to catch one of them unaware. There. I spy a lone figure picking their way through the trees—the first sign that my suspicion was off base. Still, I pivot to cut off their only escape and rush them from behind. Before I even touch them, more oddities stick out—despite being dressed in bulky, black material, they don't appear to be armed. As my arm goes around their waist, their scent hits me full in the chest. I'd know it anywhere, delicate, and soft, so out of place above the stench of smoke that I know I've gone insane.

She really did die, and now I'm seeing her ghost, dressed in some billowing black dress that spills out from a pale blue coat. Even worse, I'm holding her in my arms. That's how far my mind has wandered. The sad part is that I don't even care. If this is what insanity is, I would rather be psychotic than face anything else.

She feels so warm that I can't stop touching her, spinning her around to face me. Throughout her entire body, I can feel her pulse throbbing. Even her lips, though swollen in the pale moonlight filtering through the branches overhead, are wet and pink, but her skin...

That beautiful supple skin I once remarked belonged only on an angel, is now covered in blood.

Fresh blood.

Suddenly, her lips part. "Daze?"

Her hoarse, broken voice is what finally sinks in. She isn't a figment of my imagination. Holy fuck, she's real. Frey is alive, but barely. It's like she's blind, staring into nothing as her eyes meet mine. Even when I brush the hair from her face, she rarely blinks. When I lift her into my arms, she remains limp as if all will to fight is gone.

"I'm here, baby," I say against her scalp, stroking through her damp hair. She doesn't smell like smoke. Just fresh air, sweat, and blood. "I'm here. It's okay. You're safe. You're safe—"

Another figure appears from the shadows, but I can tell right away that they aren't a guard. However, they could still cause some damage with what looks like a stick, brandished above their head in a trembling grip.

"L-Let her go!" she shrieks, her voice barely intelligible. I don't recognize her, but, in a twisted contrast to Frey, she's wearing a filthy white dress, her dark hair loose. Judging from the frantic fear in her dark eyes, she wasn't here as some valued wedding guest.

Holy shit. Marco wasn't lying. Human trafficking seems to be one of Michael Heywood's premier side businesses. God only knows what that bastard has already done to Frey.

"Let her go!" the woman in white demands, shifting her stance to take a whack at me with her only weapon. Adjusting my hold on Frey, I raise a hand in surrender.

"I'm not here to hurt her," I say. After wracking my brain for a suitable explanation, all I can come up with is, "What the fuck happened?"

"We don't know," the woman says, lowering her stick by a fraction of an inch. "They had us in the barn, and she got us out. The house was already on fire. I just want to get the fuck out of here."

Some of the tension in my body loosens. So, Frey wasn't inside the mansion when it went up. Thank fuck for that.

Yet again, I'm forced to admit that she smells nothing like smoke. Just blood and cologne and God knows what else... *Damn it!* Touching any part of her that I can reach, I keep smoothing my hands along her back. It's only when I draw back to see her face that I realize...

She isn't hugging me in return. With her head pressed against my shoulder, she stares at nothing, her face blank, her green eyes empty. It's like I'm not even here.

"Frey? Look at me, baby." I try to get her attention by stroking her cheek. Then I wave a hand in front of her face. Shake her gently on the shoulder.

Nothing makes her so much as flinch.

"Frey? Talk to me—"

"Daze!" Ben comes from the woods, gasping for air as if he had to struggle to catch up with me. Now, I can comprehend just how fast I'd been going. Like a mindless fucking animal.

Being near Frey restores the sanity I lost the second I saw that fire. As I look back, I realize how irrational I'd been. My only option was to run headlong into an inferno to escape the pain of grief.

"I'm never letting you out of my fucking sight," I tell Frey as Ben races toward me. "You hear me? Never fucking again."

"Daze, who the fuck are you talking to... Oh—" Ben stops short when he spies Frey in my arms and the—not one, but now *two* women huddled nearby. The other must-have crept out while I wasn't looking, also wearing a filthy white gown.

Ben takes one look at them and sighs. "Jesus Christ! You'd think by now I wouldn't be surprised by what the bastard Heywood is capable of."

"Just help me get them out of here," I say, lifting Frey off her feet. The grip I have on her is so tight she would scream if she was in her right mind, but I can't let go of her.

"Come on," Ben says, gesturing back through the woods. "Damien managed to get a foothold closer to the house, but I guess it's not necessary—"

"Catherine," Frey says, her voice a faint rasp. Lifting her head, her eyes are suddenly filled with life as they focus on the house. "Catherine."

I think I recognize the name. "Catherine Heywood?"

Ben cocks his head. "That's his wife, isn't it?"

Frey doesn't say anything else, and I don't press her for more information. Instead, my arms cradle her as I turn back the way I came.

"Ben, I need to get her somewhere safe," I say. "Now."

"Okay. I'll have someone look for Catherine, okay, kiddo?" he says to Frey. "Daze, you and one of Damien's boys can take them to the warehouse. I guess we'll have to make room for three ladies instead of one—"

"Anna?" Marco tears past me, heading toward one of the girls. At the sight of him, she cries out. A heartbeat later, they're holding each other tight.

Anna. "I think that's his sister," I say in response to Ben's questioning stare. "He mentioned her before."

"Well, shit." Ben tears a hand through his hair and sighs. "Things just got interesting. Let's get everyone back before the police show up."

He rushes off to do just that, while I hold Frey in my arms, unwilling to move. She's barely been out of my sight for two days, but...

There is no way I will ever let her go again.

FIFTEEN

DAZE

LEX DRIVES me back to the warehouse with Frey, the women, and the startled reporter in tow. I barely notice him linger behind with a nervous, "I'll uh…wait in the car."

With Frey in my arms, I'm blind to everything but her as I head straight toward the makeshift bathroom fashioned out of mixed-matched materials that Damien has scavenged together.

When I get Frey into the shower and remove her filthy, bloodied dress, I feel sick to my stomach. In anticipation of what I might find, I brace myself. God, if she's hurt or if that bastard harmed her, I'll…

Track him down and kill him with my bare hands. I'll kill them all.

"Daze…"

"I'm here, baby." I crouch before her and cradle her chin against my palm. "Look at me. What do you need?"

In this place, far from that fucking house, she doesn't seem any better. She's too thin. A hollow, frail figure of skeletal bones and papery skin. I keep stroking her as if the heat of my touch will be enough to snap some life back into her.

She still doesn't speak. As she stares at me, I don't sense the broken pain I saw the first time I met her. This is different. She's colder. Harder. It's as if just two fucking days have stripped away the last vestiges of sweet, innocent Frey—but it's not as if she's drowning in grief or fear this time.

It's anger, so strong she can't think clearly. Can't breathe. She can't look at herself in the damn mirror. She doesn't even want to look at me.

"Oh, baby…" I kiss her forehead, but I'm not sick enough to take advantage of her. There is nothing worse than this kind of agony—anger so intense that you can't think about anything else. It's new to her. She was raised in that pretty, gilded cage, shielded from the dark, twisted underbelly I grew up in.

But now?

Go figure, I have no idea how to help her navigate these emotions. All I can do is run my mouth as I wash her off, inch by delicate inch.

"You had me so fucking worried. Do you realize that? I thought I'd lost you." I twist my fingers through her hair, just to make sure she's still here and this isn't some sick hallucination after all. As soft as silk, the strands caress my skin. "Don't you ever scare me like that again. You hear me? I know you've been through hell."

That much is obvious. Although the blood isn't hers, there are plenty of bruises to compensate for that, peppering her smooth, once-unblemished skin. She has been beaten, and God knows what else. When I finger a swollen welt along her collarbone, she finally looks at me.

"It's my fault," she says, her voice hard like jagged glass. "All of it. I'm the reason Catherine's dead. Those girls... It's all my fault."

Despite my better judgment, I don't counter her yet. It seems more important for her to talk than for me to comfort her. Leaning her back against the wall, I alternate between smoothing her hair and cleaning her. As if examining me for the very first time, those large, green eyes fixate on my face, seemingly endless.

And damn. There is something almost fucking unnatural about the way my cock reacts. One glance and I'm tethered to her, unable to look away. I would follow this woman to the ends of the earth if she asked me to. Then I'd pull her back from the edge and teach her a thing or two about being so damn reckless.

There's no way around it—she scared the shit out of me. I'm still shaking, heart thumping with fear. The voice coming from my mouth doesn't even sound like me, it's too deep and raspy. "You had me so fucking worried, do you realize that?" My fingers trace her cheekbones, memorizing them. "I thought I'd never see you again. It was as if you'd ripped my fucking heart out, Frey. I never want to feel that pain again."

In order to take me in fully, she blinks and tilts her head. As she watches me, it's as if she is seeing me for the first time, and I am observing her in the same way. A beautiful pair of eyes surrounded by bruised and swollen skin. She reaches out, running her fingers along the stubble on my chin. I can't stop myself from capturing those slender digits, feeling every single inch of them.

"I know you wanted me to trust you," I say, pressing my mouth to her palm. "And I do, you know that. But if you ask me to leave you again..."

I know now isn't the time for sex. As she sucks in a breath, I can't help but pull her into me anyway, pressing my cock against the curve of her belly. Her hands grip my shoulders in return, and I sense a little bit more of her old self coming back.

"I don't know if I could do that, Freylie." My lips brush her hair as I inhale her scent, blood, sweat, and all. She still smells perfect. When I run my tongue along her earlobe, she tastes even better. Like sin and salvation rolled into one. Heaven and hell. I could worship at the altar of her body for the rest of my life and become a changed man.

"I'm never letting you out of my sight, you got that?" She doesn't react when I trace a path from her ear to her nose, then down to her upper lip. The second my lips touch the bruised skin, she flinches, and I pull back, focusing on cleaning her again.

"You don't have to tell me what happened," I explain, crouching down to drag the rag between her legs. They're shaking, along with her entire body. The only mark I find is a series of gouges on her inner thigh. Nail marks. Fuck. Did the bastard hurt her in a way that went beyond the physical? I bite my tongue rather than ask—it's not my place. Not now.

My only option is to be patient and follow her lead. When she parts her legs for me, I drag the rag between them, but not further.

"You can talk to me in your own time," I continue. "I'll leave you alone tonight if you want me to—but I'm not going beyond that door. I'll—"

"I don't want you to leave." Her voice is a thin whisper as she eases a finger beneath my chin, making me look up. The look on her face is steely, her bottom lip skewered between her teeth in a way that does not convey a fragile, broken innocence. She looks like Damien did when I suggested we take on Heywood's crew head-on. Like she's itching for a fight. Aching to stab, beat, kill.

Anything to regain control.

"If you're angry at me, you should be," I tell her, my voice thick. "I should have been there sooner, no matter what. I owe you that much. Every time those motherfuckers hurt you, that's on me. If you want me to stop, I will. You can take your time—"

"I don't need sweetness right now." Her eyes well up, but they're sterner than ever as she holds her head high like the queen she is. "I don't want you to be thoughtful and kind and patient. I just..."

"Say it." I press her palm to my cheek and force her to meet my gaze. "Tell me what you need, and it's yours. Anything."

Leaning back against the wall, she sighs and closes her eyes. Her fingers stroke the side of my jawline, as if she is trying to memorize me just as I did her minutes ago. With her thumb brushing the corner of my mouth, she suddenly stops. I am willing to risk my fucking soul for her when she opens her eyes again.

Instead, she requests something far more dangerous. "I want you to fuck me," she says. "Hard. I don't want to feel anything but you."

I lose all sense of reason as my cock battles the last shred of common sense in my brain. She's traumatized and battered. A good, boyfriend, lover, whatever-we-are, would tuck her into bed with some warm milk or some shit. Tell her to wait until the morning. Be the hero.

But I know her. I know that she wouldn't ask this of me lightly, not unless...

She needed it badly enough to beg.

Unless she needed me.

And I'll be damned if I'll deny her any damn thing.

No matter what.

SIXTEEN

FREY

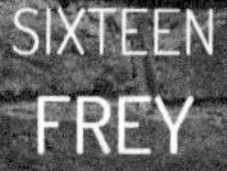

I'M adrift in my own sea of self-pity, too damn wrapped up in myself to care about anything else. Like Catherine, who may have given her life for mine. As well as Colton, who died a terrible death, and the women who just survived a far worse ordeal than mine.

I should especially care about Daze, who is practically on his knees out of concern for my well-being. But at the moment, I just feel...

Blank. Empty.

I wouldn't care if the entire world was on fire right now. I feel like a switch has been flipped inside me, numbing me to everything except helpless rage. Defeating my father is my responsibility. It was my responsibility to stop Colton sooner rather than later so that no one else had to suffer.

Maybe Daze is right, after all. In retrospect, I should have let the cards fall where they may and unleashed him on them all. This is all my fault.

"Look at me—" His voice cuts through the maddening chaos in my mind like a knife, but the clarity that follows is disorienting, like being struck over the head. It is so easy for him to make the insane seem plausible. One look from him makes me feel powerful and in control. He has me in the palm of his hand, and it should be the other way around. I should be the strong, unyielding one.

He has enough on his plate to worry about. Like Sammy, and his sister, and keeping them safe from my father's machinations.

"I don't want to be insensitive," he says, drawing out the word as if he's not used to using it. Especially not in a situation like this, with us both half-naked. "So, if you need more time, just tell me—"

"I told you what I want." My voice takes on a needy, aching quality that makes me shiver. When he doesn't move, I take his hand and press it to my belly. The heat I feel is a welcome distraction, but it stings like a bitter punishment. This isn't about pleasure.

I want him to be angry with me. I want him to convey that rage in a way that only he can. I want him to use me.

And maybe then I'll be able to feel again.

He lurches upright, his head lowered, gaze heavy-lidded. He pulls his hand out of my grasp, only to capture my waist with both. One easy shift of his body, and he has me pressed against the wall with barely any space between us.

"You want it?" His mouth grazes my ear, his voice guttural. "I didn't hear you clearly enough the first time. Say it again."

"I want you to fuck me."

He groans, flattening his hands against the wall near my head. I expect him to strip his clothes, and I start to help him, but he captures my wrist.

"You're missing something," he scolds, pressing his lips to my neck. "There was one other part you said. What was it?"

Despite everything, my lips part in a hollow imitation of a smile. "Hard. I don't want to feel anything but you."

Fabric tears as he rips the remaining shreds of my dress away. A moan travels up my throat, escaping in a gasp as he slides a finger along my inner thigh. My eyes flutter closed at the feeling, but it's just a mere taste of the oblivion I know he can give me.

Salvation in a brutal series of thrusts.

"Fuck, I'm going to hell for this," he grates out. "Spread your legs for me. Like that. Wider..."

He yanks my hips, angling me toward him as he sinks to one knee. The heat of his breath washes over me, electrifying raw, sensitive skin. I can't keep silent when he lunges, taking me fully in his mouth.

I feel fire, rippling through me, consuming me inch by inch. Then he adds a finger, stroking me from the inside out. Another. A third.

"Daze." I feel my fingers tear through his hair, desperate to guide him to where I need him the most. Ironically, he doesn't need any direction from me. It's like he can read my mind, taking his cues from the deepest, carnal impulses inside me. He knows me better than I do.

Too well.

He knows how to make my fear go away until pleasure is all I feel.

"No," I bite out, digging my nails into his skull. "I don't want this. I want—"

His teeth. I feel them rake over my flesh, and I lose track of my argument. A harsh mix of pain and ecstasy forms a bitter, painful poison. I whimper out an affirmation, and he rocks into me, using more pressure. More wet heat. More. More. More.

Then, without warning, he shoves what feels like the thickness of a thumb inside me, and I come apart at the seams.

"That's it," Daze grunts in approval. "So, fucking beautiful. You want more? I need to hear you ask for it—"

"Please."

"Good girl."

He flips me around, forcing me face-forward against the wall. His breath fans over my lower back, then lower.

"I need you to trust me, baby," he says before brushing his hand along my ass. "Trust me. Say that you do."

"I trust you." My breath feathers in and out, and it's hard to find the words to speak. Especially when I feel his thumb drift down to stroke my clit. Then up, along my ass, and back again. I jerk each time he completes a circuit. With a few simple motions, he's taken complete control of every limb and nerve. It's like his fingers are hardwired to my brain. He's a puppet master, jerking me along with invisible strings and it's all I can do just to endure.

"You're so damn wet, already," Daze says. "Fuck. You feel that, how eager you are for me?"

He taunts me, stroking me from the inside out with a crooked finger. It's a move far more gentle than what I asked for, but the second I tense, he pairs the sweetness with a harsh grind of his thumb over my clit.

"You want to do this my way?" he murmurs, watching my body jerk helplessly on the tips of his fingers. "Then I need you soaked," the exhales, teasing my flesh with another burst of prickling heat.

His tongue lashes at me with harsh, probing strokes, and I can't think. I just move and react, letting my body go on autopilot. The second I reach a sense of blank clarity...

Smack! His hand hits my ass, conveying none of the violence that Colton or my father assaulted me with. It jars me back into that clouded mindset, and before my body can even finish coming down from the brief pain, he strokes the spot with unimaginable softness.

"You feel that?" he asks me, his voice low and thick. "That's a taste of the pain you put me through. The fucking agony.

And then the memory of you that would always follow and make it so damn worth it. You are worth any pain. Do you hear me?"

I do, but somehow, the earnestness in his voice doesn't make it any easier to believe. It seems like I only cause death to those around me. I should be doing whatever it takes to atone for Catherine's death and the poor girl from the stables. I don't deserve to be in Daze's arms, let alone being pleasured by him.

I start to tense, and he must sense the change in my body before I do. Thwack! His hand strikes my inner thigh, and I jump, startled.

"Don't," he snarls, sounding feral. "For the next few moments, I don't want you to give a shit about anything or anyone but me. You got that?" He leans in, pressing an open-mouthed kiss to the curve of my hip. "In here, we're the only two things that exist. Just me and you. Fuck, you have no idea how much I missed this. The way you feel. How you smell. The sounds you make."

He drags his teeth over my skin, nipping as he goes, and I can't catch my breath. As he pulls back, I look over my shoulder, and his eyes meet mine with an intensity that makes me shiver, even before I hear him demand. "Get down. Hands and knees."

I obey him on autopilot, shuddering as my body connects with the cold, unfamiliar floor. For the first time it sinks in that I don't recognize this place. He's been busy in the short forty-eight hours that I've been gone. I want to ask him, but then I feel his fingers slide along my spine, and I lose focus again.

"Brace yourself, baby," he says, rocking into me from behind. "You wanted it rough, you got it."

I don't even have the time to second-guess my request. He heeds it perfectly, driving into me with a need that sets my body on fire. Bit by bit, I can feel the shattered, traumatized part of myself waking up, shrugging off the numb haze.

I'm not weak. I'm not an idiot for trusting the wrong people. I never should have doubted Daze.

That thought consumes me as he presses my body to the floor, his voice so guttural I can barely make out any words at all. I don't know what comes over us both, but I feel a connection to him as real and vital as my heartbeat.

He must feel it too, because his lips nudge my ear, and in a hoarse voice, he whispers, "I love you, Frey."

And just like that, he fulfilled my request in the worst possible way.

He paired agony with pleasure, just like I wanted.

DAZE

FUCK. There's something wrong with me. As I tiptoe through the darkness to find some clean clothes for us both, I have no right to feel...content. Relaxed, even. This part of the warehouse is empty—no doubt because of Ben who had greater foresight than I do, apparently. He's also the one I presume is responsible for the neat pile of clothing I find a few paces away—jeans and a shirt for me, and sweats for Frey. When we're both finally dressed, she's silent, adjusting her oversized clothing while I linger around her like a damn idiot.

"Make yourself comfortable," I choke out. Voices from the front of the building trickle back to us. It's only a matter of time before some nosy bastard wanders this way, eager to catch a glimpse of her. "I'll show you where you can sleep," I grate out.

She just nods, eyeing the remnants of that wedding dress lying in a heap on the floor. There is nothing else I can do except lead her into the back part of the warehouse, cordoned off by plywood strips nailed to support beams.

It's certainly no fancy manor but, in all honesty, *this* is the gist of what I could ever offer her—a shitty corner in a proverbial dump. The thought never used to sting like it does now. I've never felt so damn out of my element with a woman before. Even without a trace of judgment on her face, she still seems out of place. An angel who landed in hell.

"I know it's not much, but you should get some sleep," I say, inching toward the main warehouse. "There's another place we can crash at later. It'll have a bed, at least." Before I can take another step, she reaches over and brushes her hands against my chest.

"It's okay," she says, and I stop dead in my tracks. Damn. In my gut, I know she's talking about more than this. Like the fact that I spilled my guts out back there, and she said nothing in return.

Not that I expected her to. It's too fast. Renna and I rarely traded the words, and we'd been together for nearly a year before Sam came along. I'm not an expert in emotional attachment, but I think it should take longer than a couple weeks to develop something as strong as love. Right?

Wrong. It's not in my nature to play games. I know what I want when I want it. Growing up in a world where a prison sentence or bullet to the head could end your life at any moment, long-term wasn't part of my vocabulary. I'm used to fucking for one night and moving on to the next.

No one else has ever had this kind of hold over me.

I can't lie. There's something inside me that itches to lash out at her and demand an answer. *Yes,* she feels the same? *No,* she doesn't? I tell myself I can handle whatever she says, as long as she gives me *something*. Something other than a polite, blank stare I can't get a fucking read on no matter how hard I try.

"Alright, I'll let you get some sleep—"

"Wait." Her back is to me, her hair falling limply down her spine. My fingers are itching to run through it. She is so damn beautiful. My heart beats in sync with hers, bound by some invisible thread. She has me in the palm of her hand, hers to crush or destroy at a moment's notice.

And I fucking hate it.

At the same time, I can't imagine living without this bitter sting. I'm addicted to her like nothing else...

And she knows it.

"Can you stay with me?" She looks back at me through a fringe of white-blond hair. "Just for a little while."

In all honesty, the answer should be no. With Heywood's plans alone, there are so many moving parts to coordinate. Ben would kill me if he were here to see how easily I relent with a nod.

"Of course." I sink onto the narrow mattress beside her, throwing my arm around her waist. Now would be a good time to force the issue about my previous confession. I consider it.

Then I feel her body go limp in my arms, and bothering her at all becomes the furthest thing from my mind. I don't need an answer, I decide.

It doesn't matter if she feels the same way or not. I may not be an expert on love, but I can recognize it when I feel it. How she may feel in return doesn't matter.

I love Frances Heywood, and that's a fact.

Maybe she's smart enough to see that as more of a curse than a blessing.

After she's deep asleep, I finally disentangle my limbs from hers. When I step out from behind the makeshift screen, Damien is already there to block my path, arms crossed, scowl fixed.

"It's about damn time," he mutters. "I know you two needed to reconnect and all, but did you forget that you're kind of in the middle of something right now? I don't know, like tracking down a psychopath before he potentially blows up all Westpoint City to score political points?"

"Keep it down!" I glance back over at Frey. She stirs in her sleep but doesn't seem to have heard Damien, thank fuck. Still, I take a few steps toward the front of the warehouse, ensuring she's out of earshot. "But you're right," I say, turning back to Damien and Ben behind him. "So, let's get to it. Any luck tracking down where Heywood went?"

"No," Ben admits. "But your cartel buddy seems to think that he must be ready to coordinate their final plans. There is some dedication of some statue happening downtown in three days. That might be when they strike."

"And what about the fire?" I add, crossing my arms. "Any news of the stepmother?"

Damien frowns, shaking his head. "Not so much as a fucking whisper. I bet they're working overtime to keep it under wraps. They even put a notice in the paper of the princess' wedding to Mr. Burnt-n-crispy."

"Maybe now isn't the time for jokes," I point out, though sympathy for the bastard husband-to-be is far from my mind. I'm more worried about something Frey said. "Frey's step-mother could have died there too."

"My sincere condolences," Damien says with a scoff. "You know what does deserve my emotional focus right now? Getting you clear of this mess and putting Silas in check."

"Silas," I say, unnerved by a sudden realization. "He wasn't at the manor."

"No," Ben says. "Which means that Heywood thought it more prudent to have him somewhere else, tidying up loose ends."

"Sounds about right to me," Damien pitches in.

But something still doesn't add up. "How do we know that Catherine set the fire in the first place?" I counter.

Grunting, Ben strokes his chin. "You thinking it was a setup?"

"Otherwise, why would Heywood leave his daughter and new son-in-law in the middle of nowhere, unprotected? My guess is that the fire was planned to get the unfortunate new husband out of the way."

"But by who?" Ben wonders. "Silas or Heywood himself?"

"That's the real question. And how long will it take them to realize who really went up in the blaze and who didn't?"

"Another mystery to solve," Ben says with a pensive frown. "You seem to be an expert at racking them up these days."

"Well, call me fucking Nancy Drew," I counter. Hell, it's a better nickname than "ex-almost-felon." Or "murderer." In a twisted way, all this shit is squarely my fault. "The fact of the matter is that everything stems from the same two-headed snake. Silas and Heywood. We cut them off, and we slay the beast."

Ben raises an eyebrow. "So, what's our next move?"

Even though it's self-serving, I can't deny that there is some benefit to a certain approach. "We lay low," I say. "Put out feelers. Keep our heads to the ground. The men can base here, but if Frey really is essential to this whole scheme, I say we move her somewhere else. A place that's easier to defend."

Ben scoffs. "I agree, but do you have any idea where you'd like to hide the daughter of the most powerful man in the city for a few days?"

"I'll think about it," I say, heading past him toward the front of the warehouse. "Speaking of hiding, where are Lyra and Sam? You got them out of the city like I told you, right?"

Ben winces as his face turns beet red. "About that… Damien knew of a place, and it turned out to be perfectly safe. Actually, you know, it was more convenient than any other solution."

I raise an eyebrow at his cautious tone. "But?"

He shrugs. "It may or may not be legal."

"Ben…"

"Damien may or may not have had Lex hack a real estate listing for a waterfront cabin and made it so some random alias of his shows up as the owner in perpetuity."

"That definitely doesn't sound legal," I point out. Not that I'm in any position to quote property laws.

"So what?" Ben winks. "You don't really care, anyway. It can't be traced to you, either. Besides, Kane is there now, and Lex even rigged the security system so that a fly can't get close to the place without us knowing. Legalities aside, it's safe. Now we have to focus on more important things, like getting your little princess out of town."

"Any ideas?"

"I think a lakeside retreat would do her some good," he says. "But you need to get back as soon as possible. We need you if we're going to take down the Heywood bastard, not to mention Silas."

"So I take her there, but then come right back," I suggest, hating the idea almost as much as I know what a good idea it is.

"Better than putting her in harm's way," Ben replies.

I nod. But something tells me that what I want won't matter a damn bit if Frey refuses to leave.

EIGHTEEN

FREY

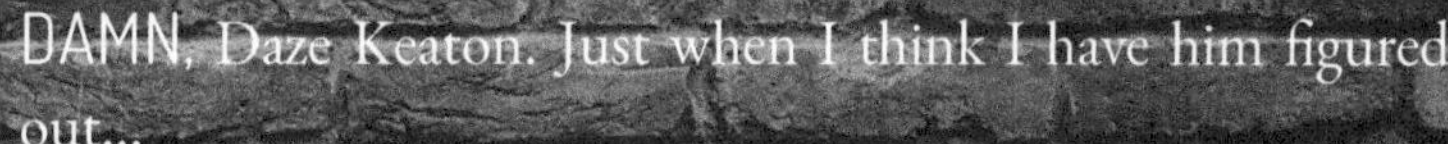

DAMN, Daze Keaton. Just when I think I have him figured out...

He has to go and say something like, *I love you, Frey.*

He meant every word—no one could deny the sincerity of his gruff tone. Daze Keaton loves me.

However, I am not worthy of that love, and I didn't even have the courage to tell him so. It isn't all self-pity that causes me to feel this way. It's a cold, hard truth. Since I met Daze a couple weeks ago, he has saved me more than once and put his life on the line without hesitation. In spite of the danger it put him and his family in, he never hesitated to take on my personal drama.

To put it simply, he is perfect.

And I would be so very selfish to continue to trap him within my web of chaos. My father will eventually have to be dealt with, and a good person wouldn't allow Daze to handle the aftermath. It seems that Michael Heywood's crimes go well beyond some petty crime ring and Hale's death. As I think of those poor girls in the barn, I know it is my duty to protect them and anyone else caught up in this maze of lies.

No matter the personal cost.

Throughout what little sleep I manage to get, the thought haunts me until a blinding white light drips through the square windows built into the corrugated metal walls as I peel my eyes open.

The place looks no better today than when I first saw it, shattered, and covered in blood. To put it politely, it's a dump. The sort of place my father's goons wouldn't dare to set up shop in. He would sneer at the dirty concrete floors and flickering fluorescent lighting, which makes me love them all the more.

With no clear direction, I slip past a gap between several large boards of plywood nailed to wooden structure beams. More makeshift planks are affixed at various intervals to divide the wide, narrow space beyond.

I don't see Daze at first. Several other equally muscular figures, wearing nondescript clothing, carry boxes from one corner to another. I wander through the perilous field of plywood, out to a broad open area where Daze sits at a long table flanked by four other figures, only two of whom I recognize.

"Looks like the princess has finally arisen," one of the men says. His shaggy dark hair and relaxed posture give away his identity even before I see his face. Ben. "Good to see you in one piece. You okay?"

I nod.

"You should still be sleeping," Daze grumbles. He pulls back from the table and approaches me. "How are you feeling?" His expression is carefully blank, and I feel a tendril of unease. Perhaps he realized over the past few hours what I already knew. I'm not worthy of his love.

"I'm okay. Have you found out anything about the fire?"

"No," he admits. "But it seems I'm not the only one in the dark."

"What do you mean?"

As he crosses over to the table, he grabs a worn newspaper from the pile strewn across its surface. The issue is from earlier this morning, and printed below the headline is a picture of a man I vaguely recognize beneath the letters: ABERNATHY Patriarch concerned about son's whereabouts.

"Colton," I say.

"This could either be a show, or it seems like your daddy hasn't been very forthcoming with his partner in crime. In any case, it gives us a good distraction to get you somewhere safe."

"Where?" I ask, curious.

He winks. "You'll see when you get there."

I wince. The secrecy triggers a chilling memory of my father blindfolding me on the way to the manor, but Daze's warm smile calms any unease. I didn't realize just how much I missed him until now. At the sight of his smile, I almost forget...

"You'll like this place, I promise," he says thickly, reaching for my hand. "I won't let anything happen to you. Do you trust me on that?"

I nod. "I trust you on anything."

NINETEEN

DAZE

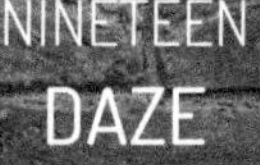

I CAN'T HELP IT. I need to see her face when we leave the city. As expected, a mixture of shock and confusion flood those beautiful damn eyes once Westpoint has faded into the distance. A swath of green spread out beneath a gray sky is all that lies ahead of us. She doesn't question me out loud, though. Instead, she keeps her gaze on the tinted windows of the truck in a subtle display of trust that blows my mind.

There is an entire police force searching for her, including her father's flunkies. Nevertheless, she can doze beside me, completely free of tension. Not for a moment do I take that trust for granted.

Damien's intel must have been spot on, because this way out of Westpoint seems clear. No one other than the average trailer or camper heading for a weekend getaway has passed us so far.

We might as well be in the middle of bum-fuck-nowhere.

As a result of the monotony, my mind starts to wander. Mainly toward Frey and her silence after my prior confession. *I love you, Frey.*

It's cliché as hell to feel this way, but it stings that she didn't say it back. Like a teenager, I was caught up in a whirlwind of hormonal affection, only to realize that the person I've been fucking only wanted that from me and nothing else. Sex.

Can I even blame her? No. Do I still want more?

Hell yes.

Call me pussy-whipped, but I would give anything in the world to hear those words trickle out of her mouth. To know that she feels the same for me. However, dwelling on it right now won't help.

As she stirs sleepily and opens her eyes, I plaster a fake fucking grin on my face.

"Hey, how you holding up?"

"I'm fine," she says, turning toward me. "Where are we going?"

I bite down on my lip and contemplate telling her the full truth or a mere summary of events. In the end, I settle for a compromise between both. "Damien knows a place just outside of town where we can lie low for a while. Knowing him, it's no luxury paradise, but I'm sure it's better than squatting behind a piece of plywood."

And, if Ben's description was anywhere close to accurate, we have to hope that the police don't catch wind of the less-than-legal means by which the place was obtained. In the meantime, it's the only safe option we've got. When I look back at Frey, she doesn't crack a smile and I sense that there's more than exhaustion to her current mood.

"What's wrong?"

"Nothing," she says, turning away. A sigh comes before I can demand a real answer. "I should be there with you, fighting to take down my father. Not sunbathing by a lake. I'm not some weak, helpless idiot. Not anymore." Her arms are crossed, and her bottom lip is caught between her teeth. It's so damn stubborn that a smile tugs on my mouth in response.

"I know that. Better than anyone, I know that."

She keeps her gaze averted away, and I know better than to push the issue.

"Look, we can talk about this later, okay?" I murmur, turning back to the road. "Besides. Looks like we're already here."

Legalities aside, Damien came through. A modest cabin is visible on a ridge near the end of a long, winding road. While it's no five-star resort, it's a step up from some shitty warehouse at the heart of a building war between the gangs and the police. It also seems to have one main access point via this very road, which I'm sure Kane has scoped out to hell and back. If the man has even a fraction of the experience he claims to, then they probably saw us coming from a mile away.

Sure enough, the second we pull up, a familiar figure appears at the end of the driveway.

"It's about damn time," Lyra mutters as I roll down the window. "I was worried sick about you. Next time, you warn me that your idea of 'safe' involves some random place in the boondocks—"

"Daddy!" A tiny figure comes running from inside the cabin at full speed. He's barefoot in bright-blue pajamas with bears printed all over them. His beaming grin is a direct contrast to the pissed, fully dressed Lyra, who looks like living hell, armed with a juice box and a cell phone.

"Sam, get back inside! I don't want you running around in this place. Be careful! And you—" Her eyes land on me, narrowed to slits. "As I was saying, it's nice to finally get a meeting with the man of the hour. You made such a show of shitting on Silas for what he dabbles in, but here I see that you've been rebuilding your own little biker gang all this time. Time you could have spent with someone else, mind you."

I grit my teeth as I park and step out of the truck. "Can we save the lecture for later?"

Lyra scoffs but shrugs. "Fine. To be fair, this place isn't too bad. The cabin itself is small, though, with just two bedrooms. Me and Sam have already claimed one and the big guy, Kane, has been taking the couch. I suppose you and your guest can decide amongst yourselves who gets the other bed."

She ushers us forward with a wave of her hand and traipses up the narrow, rickety steps to the large wooden door that serves as the main entrance. Once inside, I see that Lyra's description of the place was less than accurate—it's fully outfitted with a TV and apparently Wi-Fi, judging from the laptop that Kane has balanced on his lap while seated on a plaid couch. Not to mention, air conditioning keeps the place at a comfortable temperature, unlike the sweltering warehouse we've held up in.

"Hey, Daze." Kane acknowledges me with a nod while barely taking his eyes off the computer screen. "I've been keeping an eye out. No trouble so far."

I return his nod while still following Lyra. Past him are the two rooms with a view of the water.

"You can take that one," I say to Frey, nodding to the narrow bed. "I'll crash on the porch to keep watch."

"And I will heat up some dinner for everyone," Lyra says with a nervous laugh. Hospitality isn't in her nature—she must be anxious as hell, more worried than she's letting on. To my shock, she even musters up a wary smile before returning to the kitchen.

In no time, we're all settled in and seated around the rickety table in the main room. Kane is nowhere in sight, though I notice Lyra set a plate of warmed spaghetti aside.

"You seem to be in a good mood," I point out before taking a bite. The taste of homecooked food makes me realize just how fucking long it's been since I've tasted anything resembling a decent meal. Too long.

Even Frey starts in on her plate of food with earnestness. Damn. I catch myself staring, and I nearly miss the moment Sammy reaches across the table for me. At least not until his fork flies from his grasp and strikes me full in the face.

"Sorry, Daddy!" he chirps, flashing an impish grin. As long as it's been since I've had good food, it's been even longer since I sat down to eat with him at all. He still hasn't gotten the hang of utensils yet. There is more sauce smeared around his mouth than in it, I suspect. With a playful sigh, I grab a napkin and attempt to clean him up, while he squirms to shake me off.

"No! I'm a big kid now. I can do it myself!" He pries the napkin from my hand and winds up just making an even bigger mess.

I sit back and watch him, laughing my ass off. At the same time, a deep sense of guilt hits me straight in the gut. I've missed too many damn moments like this. Too many.

"Why are you sad, Daddy?" Sammy asks. His smile falls, and his eyes widen. "What happened to your face?" he asks Frey next. "You have boo-boos everywhere."

"It's nothing," she says with so much false cheer I almost believe her.

"I'm not sad," I say before Sam can question her further. I reach out to stroke my fingers through his wild mess of blond hair. "I'm happy. Very happy. I get to hang out with you for a while."

"Really?" His eyes sparkle, and he turns his attention to Frey. "Even you, Ms. Lady?"

I hold my breath, unsure of how she'll react. Not that I should have been worried. If there is one thing she knows how to do, it's put on a show and flash a good-girl smile, even if she's destroyed on the inside. She does so now for my son's benefit. Damn. I didn't think it was possible to feel more gratitude for her than I already do. She makes herself put on a veneer of happiness just for him, erasing all traces of sadness from her face.

"Yes," she says, matching his excitement. "We can do whatever you want."

Sammy's eyes go even wider. In an awed tone, he whispers, "Bedtime story?"

"Yeah," I say, wincing. How long has it been since I've read him one of those? I don't even want to know.

"I packed his favorite book," Lyra calls from the counter. Her back is turned, but I know her ears are perked, primed to hear every word. "It's in the room."

"Alright, then!" I slam a hand onto the table. "When you finish eating, we'll get to it."

Sammy shoves one last bite of pasta into his mouth. Then he flashes a messy grin. "Done!"

I help him into the small bathroom to brush his teeth and finally clean his face. Then I carry him into the room he shares with Lyra and tuck him into the narrow bed. He watches me expectantly, his hands folded over a blue comforter that I draw up to his chin. "The monkey book," he prompts, nodding toward a corner of the room where his bag of things is. Frey moves first and retrieves the requested book about a family of monkeys sharing a bed.

As I prop the book open on my lap, I go all in while reading it. I do different voices for each character, and repeat his favorite lines to his heart's content. He makes me reread the entire book three times before he finally drifts off.

When I look over at Frey, she's watching me, her expression unreadable. The brave face she put on around Sam has fallen. She seems lost again. Too damn delicate to pester with questions now.

"You should get some sleep," I say, as I stand and lead the way into the hall. "You can take the other room. I'll keep watch."

I head for the front of the cabin, expecting her to stay back, ready to continue our conversation tomorrow. At least that gives me more time to think of a way to question her without sounding like a thoughtless dick. I'm so fixated on the thought that I pass the main room of the cabin and barely notice that Kane has returned, eating his food alongside a suddenly chatty Lyra. I offer up a grunted greeting, but as I step outside, I expect to be alone for the first time in hours. Instead, the second I set foot onto the porch, someone too short to be Lyra or Kane is right on my heels.

"Damien is going to send one of his boys out here to keep watch," I say. "You'll be safe."

"But *you* won't be," she counters.

"Look, we don't have to talk about what happened back there," I say, even though the curiosity is killing me. I can't stop replaying the worst-case scenarios in my head. The bruises on her face don't put my fears at ease any, not to mention the scratches on her inner thigh...

God, if that motherfucker wasn't already dead...

I'd kill him myself.

"But I need you to know, that it's not easy for me to just sit on my fucking hands while you tiptoe in and out of danger. It's not, Frey. It fucking... It kills me to know you're in danger."

She sits on the step beside me, but not close enough to touch. Wearing my clothing, she looks so damn delicate, shrouded in gray cotton. I can't stop myself from reaching for her, pressing my hand over her shoulder. Despite the tension between us, she doesn't shrug me off. Thank God for that. Our reunion last night did little to ease the ache I feel without her. It's more than lust, deeper than pure sex. I need to feel her skin on mine. Taste her.

But I'd be a fool to overstep, especially when she made her feelings more than clear. She doesn't see this as a serious thing. The strange part? I feel like I could be okay with that, just as long as it meant that she stuck around.

"You can hate it if you want, but I give a shit about what happens to you." I start to pull my hand away, but her fingers seize my wrist, holding my palm captive against her. Fuck. I breathe out through gritted teeth, and it takes all the willpower I have to keep from pulling her against me.

"I don't hate it," she admits, her voice so soft I have to lean in to hear her. "I just don't want you thinking that I'm some fragile little girl who can't handle herself."

"I know you're not," I tell her. "Hell, I still have the bite marks to prove it."

That draws a smile out of her, and I don't restrain myself from touching her any longer. I sweep my thumb along the corner of her mouth. She sucks in a breath, and I feel a jolt through my body, electrifying every nerve.

I don't know who moves first, but when I'm kissing her, nothing else in the world matters. Just her scent. Her taste on my tongue. Hungry for more, I pin her down against the steps. My hands roam her body, desperate to feel as much of her as I can. She reaches for me, just as impatient. I feel her hands slip beneath my shirt, and I groan.

Suddenly, a noise comes from inside the house. It sounds like Lyra, still talking to Kane. Judging from the intermittent laughter that follows, he's one of the few people in the world to crack her shell. Odd.

But that also means she's awake, liable to hear any sound we make out here.

"Damn," I whisper. The point is, fucking on the porch probably isn't the most private location.

Frey starts to pull away, her cheeks pink, but I let my dick do the talking. My eyes latch onto the truck, and when I stand, she's on my heels. We scramble into the back seat, and I pull her beneath me with mindless need. Having her ride me is sexy as hell, no less enjoyable than plain ol' fucking.

But in this moment, I need to be on top and press her body into the leather seat beneath. I need to have the leverage to rock into her so deep her eyes go back in her head. I need control.

Because something tells me, that where she is concerned...

I won't have it for very long.

Already, she grapples for my hips, pulling me into her. Soon, she alone sets the pace, and I'm just along for the fucking ride. Not that I would have it any other way.

She feels like heaven, gripping me like a vice, moaning into my ear as if nothing else in the world matters but this.

"That's it," I tell her, my voice thick. "No one's here to see you, Freylie. Show me what you need."

Me. Me with my cock buried to the hilt inside of her. More, demanded with throaty gasps issuing from her throat and her nails sinking into my skin. She doesn't give a damn if she hurts me or not. I don't want her to.

"That's it," I say into the crook of her neck as I feel her body quiver around me. "You're mine, Frey. All mine. I can feel you coming—"

And as if my voice is a lit match, she goes up in flames. Her head flies back, hips arching against the leather upholstery, eyes wide, bottom lip clenched between her teeth. She is so fucking beautiful, and a sense of possession slams into me like a freight train. Brutally. Punishingly.

Perfectly.

When I go limp, softening inside of her, I know without a fucking doubt that it doesn't matter who stands in our way —Heywood, Silas, anyone.

No one will ever come between us.

Never again.

FREY

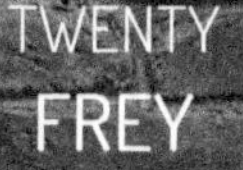

I WAKE up in Daze's arms, slumped over the back seat of a truck, to the thump of a tiny hand banging on the window near my head. Within seconds, my confusion disappears as the memories of last night come flooding back.

Mainly the understanding that Daze and I aren't alone on this adventure.

"Daddy, wake up!" Sammy's voice commands, muffled from beyond the window glass. "Auntie Lyra made breakfast! Wake up!"

"I'm awake," Daze grumbles, his mouth pressed against my shoulder. He sighs and reaches blindly for his jeans. "I'll distract the tiny human. You go shower and get dressed."

Before I can agree, he lurches upright and rolls down the window enough to shout, "Hey, buddy! Think you can race me back inside and hide somewhere where I can't find you? Bet you can't!"

Sammy's reply is an excitedly chirped, "Yes, I can!"

"Time bought," Daze says with a smile. I shiver as he turns the full force of that expression on me. He is so beautiful, sometimes it hurts to meet his gaze head-on. Like standing in the path of an oncoming truck moving at full speed. There is no chance to react before...

Boom. You're crushed against the onslaught.

I barely notice he's moved until I feel him help me back into my shirt. Then he yanks my sweatpants back into place. Once he's dressed, he leaves the truck and guides me up the path to the cabin and safely into the narrow bathroom before he sets off to find Sam.

I wash up blindly and then hunt for my bag of borrowed clothing. After getting dressed in a clean shirt and jeans, I find myself wandering in the main room, with Daze and Sammy nowhere in sight. Confused, I head outside and start down the porch steps.

When I hear a voice call out, I turn around in time to catch a small cherub-like figure running to greet me with outstretched arms.

"Ms. Lady!"

"Sammy?"

I stoop to catch him mid-hug, and I squeeze him tight.

"I'm so glad you're okay, honey," I tell him, smoothing back his blond curls. "Do you know where your daddy is?"

"Yeah!" He tugs me along behind the cabin, where a massive Daze is attempting to "hide" behind a narrow tree. As Sammy and I approach, he makes a show of lunging toward us, growling playfully.

Giggling, Sammy tries to outrun him, and they play a haphazard game of tag throughout the narrow clearing. Finally, Daze throws up his hands in surrender.

"I give up! Let's go eat, little man," he declares before lurching to scoop Sammy into his arms. Sammy's elated giggles form a trail all the way to the cabin.

I follow behind them, unable to shake the feeling that something is off. Daze has been distracted ever since we left the city, not that I can blame him. If I were in his position, I'd pester me until I got an answer.

I can tell he's dying to ask what happened with Colton and Catherine. I should tell him, but there is this selfish part of me that doesn't want his opinion of me colored by that. Will he judge me for what I had to do to survive? Or will he hate me for letting Catherine sacrifice herself so easily without putting up a fight?

The questions haunt me as I enter the cabin and find Lyra in the kitchen, slaving over the stove. Daze leans against the wall, already eating a pancake with his bare hands, while Sammy watches him from a round table, clapping in delight.

"Oink oink, that's the sound a piggy makes!" Sammy cackles gleefully as Daze proceeds to make those very sounds on command. "Yay!"

"Don't forget to eat your own food, little piggy," Lyra scolds, crouching to cut his pancake into pieces. Looking up, she spots me and nods toward the counter. "I made you a plate. You're probably starving."

"Thank you."

Daze staggers to right himself, still smiling in a way that makes my heart flutter. He's so beautiful like this, consumed only with the task of entertaining his son.

"Here." He moves to pull out a chair for me, and I grab a full plate and sit across from Sammy, who has syrup dripping down his chin.

"Daddy said we can go play in the water!" Sammy sings. "Wanna come?"

"I said we can walk by the water," Daze corrects, his voice gently stern. "It's not safe to go in."

"We can walk," Sammy insists, batting his golden eyelashes. "Wanna come?"

"Of course." I muster up a smile in return. "If you'll have me."

"Yay!" Sammy starts to push back from the table, but Lyra calls from the other side of the kitchen.

"You need to eat first, young man. Then you can go out and play."

"Okay!" Sammy painstakingly eats the rest of his food while Daze and I trade silent glances from over the table.

I don't know how to describe the way he looks at me. His gray eyes sparkle, open and warm—but the thoughtful tilt to his mouth conveys a vulnerability that makes my heart ache. What happened between us last night has only made the unspoken tension between us more awkward. I feel like I'm going to explode by the time Sammy finishes up and Daze takes a quick shower. When we finally head outside, the sun is shining high in the sky and the chaos in the city seems to be a world away.

Sammy takes off, bounding over the paths that lead to the lakefront. It's secluded out here, which is surprising for such a beautiful location. I assume the weather has something to do with it. It's chilly, and Daze has to scold Sammy more than once to keep him from touching the water.

To his credit, the boy responds to every warning with a firm nod and a cherub grin. Cheeky. I can tell already that he'll grow up with more than his fair share of Daze's penchant for bending the rules. For good or bad? That remains to be seen.

Eventually, the three of us sit on a rocky outcrop and watch the waves lap at the shore. I'm not sure exactly when it happens, but when I look over at Sammy, he's fast asleep with his head on Daze's shoulder.

I don't know why now feels as good a time as any to broach the topic, but with a heavy breath, I confess, "Nothing happened between me and Colton. I didn't let him touch me." Raw anger creeps into my voice, and a deep understanding crosses over Daze's features.

He nods once. "Good. Are you ready to tell me what else happened out there?"

My voice breaks as I tell him everything, checking periodically to make sure Sammy doesn't wake up in the middle of the horrible retelling. I tell him about my father's threats and Silas' visit. Then of Colton. As my voice breaks, Daze takes my hand in a firm fist, silently urging me to continue. When I reach the part about the girl, however, he hisses, visibly disgusted.

"Those sick sons of bitches..."

"No, I should have done something," I insist. "I should have done more. Fought back. Anything but run away like a scared little girl."

Yet again.

Self-pity almost swallows me whole—until I look up and catch the fire in those beautiful gray eyes that hold my own without flinching.

"The hell you could," he snaps, his voice rough. Suddenly, he grips my hand tighter while stroking the back of it in a way that makes my heart twist into knots. He can be so gentle when he wants to be, despite the harsh callouses that mar nearly every inch of his palms. He softens his grip without seeming to think about it, as if he's painfully aware of his effect on people. It's a marked sign of humanity that Silas, Colton, my father, and anyone like them doesn't possess. "You fought back, but you're one damn person. I'm just thankful as hell that you made it out in one piece."

"But my father is still out there," I say. "Who knows what he's doing. God, those poor girls…"

"That's not all he's up to," Daze says darkly.

I look at him questioningly, but he hesitates to respond. After checking one more time to make sure Sammy's asleep, he cradles his son's head with so much tenderness it hurts to witness.

"Your father's plans don't end with his fucked-up little cult," he says. "There's more to it."

"Like what?"

"He wants to blow up the entire city."

I blink, unsure of how to interpret that. Am I surprised? Maybe. The word choice is rather blunt, but somehow, I doubt that Daze is exaggerating. I can sense the tension he's tried so hard to hide all along. This is the real reason he's been on edge since we left Westpoint.

"How?" I stammer. "And when?"

"We're not sure of the finer details," he admits with a heavy sigh. "But the intel is credible. It's going to happen soon. Probably during his little victory speech at city hall."

"We have to stop him," I say, already wracking my brain as to the many potential ways my father could utilize his newfound power to sow chaos—not to mention the untold damage he could do with someone like Silas as his attack dog.

I lurch to my feet, and head toward the truck we arrived here in.

"We need to go. Now—"

"Wait." I look back to see Daze cradling a dozing Sammy in his arms. With a pleading expression, he jerks his chin to the cabin. "Just give me a minute."

Reminded of reality, I deflate of some of the urgent tension driving me to move now. Act now. Instead, I swallow hard and follow Daze into the cabin. We pass his sister and the hulking man he referred to as Kane seated at the dinner table. Once inside the farthest bedroom, Daze gingerly tucks Sammy into bed. He lingers, smoothing his fingers along his son's mop of blond hair. My heart aches watching him. It's hard to remember that these hands—capable of violence— can be so gentle as well.

I turn around, feeling like a voyeur watching what should be a private moment. Daze is on my heels before I can even blink. Warm, he uses his body to encase me from behind, cupping my waist in the palm of each hand. Then he steers me outside and down the porch steps.

"Hold on," he murmurs into the nape of my neck as we stand still on the earthen path leading to the road. "Nothing good can be accomplished by rushing in there, guns blazing."

But that's the exact M.O. he's stuck to since the moment I met him.

Unless all the head trauma he's taken in the past few days has caused lasting damage, I can't imagine why he'd call for tact now.

Unless...

He doesn't want me with him when he finally does return to the city.

Even worse—he thinks I can't stomach one last showdown with my own father.

TWENTY-ONE

DAZE

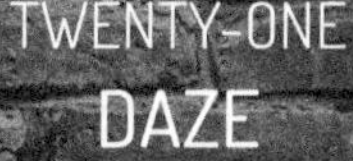

SHIT. I've done it now. Can't say I feel too much guilt though. From where I'm standing, nose buried in a mess of wild, blond hair, my original plan is seeming like a damn good reason.

Until Frey wriggles away from me and spins around, head cocked at an accusatory angle.

"We have to go back," she insists. "*We*. I have to stop my father. Why didn't you tell me sooner?"

"We weren't sure," I admit. "And you had just gotten out of that fucking mess. You didn't need anything else on your plate."

"Don't make decisions for me. We're a team, remember?" She says it so hesitantly, like she isn't sure. Like she thinks I'll balk at the idea of having my fate lumped in with hers.

She's damn wrong.

I grip her wrist, pull her into me, and press my lips to hers, catching her off guard. When I draw back, her eyes are heavy lidded, all traces of irritation gone.

"You're damn right, we are," I say, meaning every single word. "We can handle this together. But if you think that I'm letting you anywhere near that city when there's a possibility that it, and everyone in it, could go up in smoke..." I hear the shift in my voice, and so does she. I watch her body tense before I say, "You've lost your damn mind. I almost lost you more than once already. You have another thing coming if you think I'm going to take that risk again."

And I refuse to feel an ounce of guilt over that. Still, I grit my teeth as she frees her wrist from my grasp.

"It's not your risk to take," she says softly, turning away.

I inhale sharply. Now isn't the time to launch into some deep emotional bullshit, but... Fuck it. We've both beaten around the bush for long enough. I need to know.

"I love you, and you think that means I shouldn't have any say over whether or not you risk your life? That's a bit fucked up, Frey."

She stiffens. Sucks in a startled breath. Exhales. "Daze..."

"Look, I don't care if you feel the same way or not," I add. It's the fucking truth. "But that doesn't mean I can sit back and watch you die. I can't. I won't."

Her eyes meet mine. "I do love you," she says. "That's why I won't sit back and let you take all the fire by yourself. That wouldn't be fair to you."

My mind is blown. I forget all about our conversation but those four words. *I do love you.*

So what if there aren't fireworks or other romantic bullshit to cushion the blow? I'd crawl over broken glass just to make her say those words again.

For the time being, I settle for reaching out, ghosting my fingers along her shoulder. "You love me," I echo, my voice low. "Well, that's nice to fucking hear."

Finally.

"As if it matters," she says, keeping her face turned away from me. "All I've done is get you and Sammy into danger."

"Well, guess what? It's not your risk to take. It's mine."

And when it comes to my life, I'd risk it again and again for her. Sammy has Lyra to take care of him should the worst come to worst—not that I would ever willingly let that happen.

"It doesn't hurt that I've proven damn hard to kill," I point out.

That makes her look back at me, and I suck in a breath at the sight of her—eyes questioning, bottom lip trapped between her teeth. "Well, then it seems like we're at an impasse," she admits. "We could fight about it. But..."

"But?" I take a step toward her without realizing it. Damn. It's like she has my heart in a vice, balanced on the palms of those delicate hands. I'm hanging on every second of silence that passes between us. For the rest of my fucking life, it's going to be like this. Waiting for her say-so over every little thing.

I could live with that—with no regrets, either. It blows my mind to admit it, but I don't dare second-guess myself. Even if Damien would hiss that I was *pussy-whipped*.

"Fine," I say through clenched teeth. "We'll do this together—"

Her eyes widen and I know I made the right choice. Even if I hate the prospect of putting her in danger, I hate the thought of disappointing her more.

"But," I add. "I'm not letting you out of my fucking sight."

She interprets that condition with a curt nod, but some of the tension leaves her body. Damn. It's like we both can breathe again. I take her hand in mine again, pulling her close. This time, she doesn't pull away. It's only when I feel her start to shiver in the cool night air that I remember we're standing outside, in the middle of nowhere.

"We still have things we need to discuss," I tell her, leading her outside.

I pull her down the path until the trees shield us from view but leave a clear line of sight to the cabin. Then I turn to face her, and grab her by the waist.

"There's something important we need to square away before we talk about any other shit dealing with your father."

"What?"

"I'm going to need you to repeat that last part again," I say. "Before we were interrupted?"

Her eyelids lower as she sucks in a tiny, startled breath. Then something comes over her, empowering her to tilt her head back to meet my gaze head-on, without an ounce of fear.

"I love you," she says.

"That's damn right. Say it again."

"I love—"

My lips seal over hers, and I inhale the confession like it's a fucking lifeline, and I've been drowning up until this point. All my life, I never realized the power of those three fucking words. How they can make a man feel when uttered in a broken whisper by a woman who sets his soul on fire.

Here, in the middle of nowhere, shrouded by trees, I feel like the richest man on the planet, unable to be knocked down by anyone else.

"Again," I tell her, when I finally let us both come up for air. "I need to hear you say it."

"I love you." Her words end with a moan as I press her back against the nearest tree. "Daze, Keaton..."

I sink to my knees, feeling like I'm at an altar, ready to confess my sins, and an angel is there to greet me, all I have to do is bare my soul.

And I'll gladly give her everything.

My lips find her thigh as I peel down her borrowed sweats and wrench up the oversized shirt. Each glimpse of her skin feels like the very first time all over again. I knew back then that there was more to what had sparked between us than a grimy one-night stand in my old man's gym. I knew from the second I saw her on the bridge, her face upturned to the sky, ready to submit to whatever fate had in store for her, that this woman would grab me by the balls, and I'd have no say in it.

"I love you," I hear her breathe out the second I let my lips come into contact with the sweet strip of flesh in between her thighs.

"I love you," I say, letting my voice easily overpower hers. It feels important for me to say it, over and over so that she can't doubt me. Not for a damn second.

I love her even if I don't understand the emotion beyond what I feel for Sam and my sister. I need her in a way that feels integral to my very being.

"Frey Heywood, I love you, even if you come to hate me. I always will."

No matter what we'll both have to go through to take her father down, I feel in the pit of my soul that I won't hesitate when it comes to protecting her.

No matter what has to be done in the end.

Her hand tugs impatiently at my hair, cutting off my internal shitty monologue. Like a servant at her disposal, I turn my attention to showing her the way I feel physically. I make her come so many times her knees are shaking by the time I finally pull back.

Then I strip her down to nothing and watch her body come alive, too far gone to give a damn for modesty. This is the way she's meant to be viewed. In utter confidence, by the only man she deems worthy of having her.

The power in that isn't lost on me. I know what it means for her to have chosen me, even if she thought I was a worthless punk. She saw through that in an instant. Somehow, she still seems to see right through me, to the person I didn't even know existed underneath.

He's a strange motherfucker, this new Daze Keaton. Someone I doubt I could see myself ever being, just a year ago. A man who puts his heart above all else.

And doesn't regret one damn thing.

When we head inside the cabin, Kane and Lyra are once again seated at the kitchen table. She throws her head back and laughs at something he must have said before we came in.

"And I thought I had it rough with one puking toddler to chase around. How on earth did you do it with twins?"

"Easy." Kane chuckles and sips from a chipped mug, filled with what looks to be coffee. "By the grace of God," he says. "Doing another tour in the army would be ten times easier, but I wouldn't trade them for the whole world."

"And you said they both live with your ex?" Lyra asks, but for once, her voice lacks the condescending tone I'm used to her using when it comes to me. "How old are they now?"

"Ten," Kane says. "But I still see them as crazy little runts running around with full diapers."

"I'll drink to that! I feel the same way about my own son." Lyra sips from her mug, still smiling, and for a second, I wonder if Silas and Heywood's grand plan was to have her body snatched with some less-uptight clone.

"Nice to see you two have been bonding," I say from the doorway.

Lyra scowls, instantly proving she's the same sister I know and love.

"I'm going to stay here and keep these three company," Kane says. "Damien and the others aren't far. You'll meet there to discuss the finer points of the plan."

I can feel Frey's eyes burning a hole through the back of my neck. "It'll be just Sam and Lyra staying here," I clarify. "Frey's coming with me."

Kane raises an eyebrow, but if he objects to her presence, he has enough tact not to say so out loud. "It's your crusade, man," he says with a nod. "We're just along for the ride."

"Along for the ride while sitting in the driver's seat," I point out, pulling out a chair. "We should go over the plan in detail."

Kane nods and reaches into his pocket for a cell phone. How in the hell he manages to get service all the way out here? I'll never know. Still, he places it on the table and pulls up a grainy photo of a map of Westpoint City. "Damien sent this over. He marked where the speech will be and—"

"I think this is my cue to excuse myself," Lyra says, heading for the door to the porch. Judging from the way she pats the pocket of her jeans, she has a pack of cigarettes in there, ready to be chain-smoked.

As she leaves, I beckon Frey closer. "You still want to be included?"

Her eyes flash with determination. "Yes."

We go over the finer details of our supposed grand plan, until Sam wakes up from his nap and emerges from the bedroom.

"Why?" he demands when I tell him that I'll be heading back to the city. "Why can't I come too?"

"Because I need you here to protect your Auntie Lyra."

He takes in that request with a solemn nod. "Okay, but when you come back, you, me, and Ms. Lady, we'll go play in the lake, right?"

"You, me, and Frey will go walk by the lake," I say, ruffling his hair.

When we leave, I feel a pang in my chest that I don't expect. It lingers as Frey and I pile into the truck and worsens as I pull out of the driveway. By this time tomorrow, we will either be living out Sam's fantasy, or...

He'll be down one less parent. Hell, he's young enough that he might not even process the difference right away. Maybe that's for the best. I'm not oblivious to my absence in his life. Lyra has been more of a father to him than I've been lately, but that doesn't mean I'm not ready to rectify that.

I am. I want to be in his life fully without worrying that my past mistakes will catch up to me and take me away from him again. I want to be there for my son one hundred percent of the time.

I will be that for him, God as my witness.

And it wouldn't hurt to have a calm, beautiful woman by my side.

"I know you're worried," Frey says as if she can read my mind. She leans into me, hooking her delicate fingers around my own. "I am, too."

"Me, worried?" I scoff, but when I glance out of the corner of my eye, I can tell she's not buying the act. Then it hits me that if I want this to work, I can't rely on bravado alone. Honesty must come into the equation at some point.

"Frankly, I'm wondering what it will take for me to convince you to go back and stay at the cabin. It's too dangerous. I told you what your father has in store. You can bet that even having you within the city won't change his mind."

"I know," Frey says. Then she tilts her head, and I can see her brows furrow. She's thinking hard about something. Damn. I've forgotten how beautiful she looks like this, bottom lip trapped between her teeth, gaze turned inward.

I can't stop myself from asking, "What are you thinking?"

She sighs. "I'm thinking... What if he *did* know I was in the city?"

"I hate to be the one to say it, but if you're expecting some sudden change of heart because you're his daughter, that seems a little farfetched. Nothing he's done up until now seems to faze him."

"I know. That's because he thinks he's in control," she says, pressing her lips together in a thoughtful line. "But I keep thinking about something Silas told me..."

"Oh?" My vision threatens to turn red at the thought of that bastard coming anywhere near her. Over my dead body. "I hope that doesn't mean what it sounds like."

She shrugs, her gaze wistful rather than fearful. "He said that it appeared my father was in control, as if he knew something that we didn't. Then, with the fire and everything... I have to wonder if he isn't gunning to stage an outside ploy all along. What better time to strike than right when my father thinks he has a win sewn up and the levers of power on a silver platter?"

"You think Silas might be aiming to disrupt the grand explosion? How? I know the bastard better than you do, and taking credit for the work of another is his M.O."

"I'm not sure," Frey says softly. "Maybe there's more to it than my father realizes. Maybe the bombs are planted in a different location than where he thinks? I mean, why would

Silas do his bidding perfectly? My guess is he wouldn't. He has to have a backup plan."

"I hate to break it to ya, but Damien and his boys scoped it out. The shit seems to be set in the concrete used by Higher Limit. Hard to prove even if Heywood didn't own the cops, and it's too soon to stop what's in motion anyway. All we can do is try to keep anything from detonating."

A task easier said than fucking done.

She's silent for a long time, still thinking, and my dick twitches at the sight of her. She's never been more beautiful than she is now, with her intelligence on full display. There's something I missed, but she hasn't.

"You aren't convinced," I say, inferring what her silence means. "Talk to me."

"What if those aren't the only locations of the bombs?" she says. "What if, there is more of the city under attack than my father realizes?"

I frown, thinking it over. The plan is already risky from a logistical standpoint. Explosions mean fire and fire is hard as hell for anyone to control. Especially if Heywood's aim is to enact some twisted version of Marshall law that will allow him to take over the city.

Unless...

"City hall," I say. "It was on the list, but there was no construction date. I thought it was just there to mark where Heywood would be, but..." Son of a bitch. Why didn't I see it sooner? "What if Silas is planning to hit there?"

I wouldn't put it past him, the son of a bitch. Hell, it's just like him—lure his so-called partner into a false sense of security. Then strike like the sneaky bastard he is.

Frey's eyes widen, her jaw tight. "That would be total chaos. It would be—"

"Anarchy," I finish for her. "Which is Silas' fucking middle name. You might be right. The bastard could be planning to wipe out all the power in the city in one fell swoop. We have to find a way to evacuate the city or—"

"Maybe we beat them at their own game," Frey says softly. "We call their bluff."

I glance at her so sharply that I nearly drive us both off the road. At the last minute, I right the wheel, thankful that the highway is mostly empty. "You're not saying what I think you are? That we let the city explode with us and countless people in it?"

"No." She looks at me with that confident gleam in her eye, and I instantly feel like an idiot for doubting her. "But what if we take advantage of the moment to expose the reality behind my father's lies and Silas' greed?"

"How? You want to use your reporter friend and try to get it in the paper or some shit? It's a smart idea, but I don't think we have the time."

"Not in a newspaper," she says, her voice soft. "We go directly to the news station and jam the broadcast. We expose everything that my father is planning in detail, in real time."

"Yeah, but he'll be broadcasting around the same time. Besides, there's no way in hell anyone will believe it without proof."

"We don't need proof," she insists. "We simply need to buy time and get my father and Silas to see each other's true colors. Turn on each other. If we can stave off the detonation and seed doubt, they'll do the rest. Silas himself even told me a salient piece of advice." Her cold, hard smile reveals that she isn't looking back on these words fondly. "Pride cometh before the fall. We let them both revel in their victory and then force them to watch it collapse before their very eyes."

"Well, I'll be damned," I say, feeling my lips quirk into a smile. "Sounds like I've been rubbing off on you."

"There's one part of my plan I don't think you're going to like," she adds before I can gloat too much. "For this to work, it can't just be anyone on the broadcast. It needs to be me."

And she saw the same fucking map I did.

Among most of the lower side, one building in particular stands in the path of a potential bomb. The news station.

And she wants to place herself there, right at the most pivotal moment of this entire crazy scheme.

Right when all our lives will be on the line.

I want to refuse outright. Scream at her, *hell no*. Riot. Argue. Fight.

Instead, I look her in the eye, and I don't see the same frightened woman who once tried to jump off a bridge. I see a fighter. Someone who is more than capable of holding her own, no matter the risk.

Someone I'd be a selfish bastard to hold back.

So, I nod, just once. "It better be a convincing fucking speech."

DAZE

RETROSPECTIVELY, the plan makes sense. Damien and his boys deactivate the bombs scattered throughout the city, while we draw Heywood out into the open. Bada bing, bada boom. We've saved the city and stopped creepy asses from taking over.

Simple.

Until Frey and I arrive and see just how complicated a plan like that will be to pull off, on today of all days. What on the map had seemed like a few blocks, was now a maze of redirected traffic and a few dozen police cordons blocking off whole swaths of the downtown.

Moses himself couldn't part this logistical mess without breaking a sweat. Even a bastard as crazy as Damien will have his work cut out for him.

"We're going to be stretched thin," Damien warns as we pull into a vacant lot just outside the city center. He's dressed in black, a dark hood pulled low over his face. Not that anything could disguise the crazy-ass gleam in his eyes. "There's no time to fuck around," he adds. "We need to move in and out."

"Got it," I reply, but Damien holds up a hand.

"There's more. You know the boys I sent to tail Silas? They aren't answering."

No wonder he's already itching for a fight. "Shit."

"We need him out of commission," Damien warns. "Unless we want this whole plan to blow up in our faces. Literally."

And something tells me that Silas is well aware of just what is at stake. He'll hide with his tail between his legs until it's safe to show his face. Unless...

Unless someone acts as bait to draw him out into the open.

"I'll go and head him off," I say. Then I catch a pair of bright eyes, watching me warily. "But then, who will go to the station? Frey isn't going out there alone—"

"I have to," she counters, raising her voice over mine. "I can do this. I need to."

A sigh rips from me. "I don't want to fucking argue." But to protect her, I will. "I can't let you do this. Not alone."

Though it doesn't seem to matter one damn bit what I think. Those blue eyes are steely, fixed with determination. "It's the only logical choice. You can't be in two places at once, and there's not enough time to argue. I'm going."

"There's always another option," Ben says, appearing by Damien's side. "You draw Silas in. She exposes her father. Not to be cliché, but I think there is a way to kill two birds with one stone."

"How?" I ask, though I already know the answer.

Even before he shrugs and says, "You take her to the station and make a big enough scene to catch Silas' notice. No matter the risk, he won't be able to resist confronting you face-to-face. You know that as much as I do."

That idea sounds worse than leaving Frey unguarded. Putting her right in the middle of a figurative firefight?

I shake my head. "Fuck no."

"Think about it," Ben insists in that eerily calm voice that can make walking out in a blizzard seem like a good idea. "You track down Silas to contain him, and then what? Unless you have good intel, by the time you track him down, it might be too late. But with this... I could see Heywood using him to hunt down his precious little girl. It will raise fewer questions than if the cops do it, and they'll be preoccupied anyway. He'll send in Silas."

"You have a point," I admit.

"And," Ben adds. "Depending on where Silas is, it could take him longer to get there than anticipated. That could throw the timeline off. I doubt Heywood wants him blown up."

"And me and my boys will handle the rest," Damien says. "You just buy us enough time. Spread some fucking chaos."

"Okay." I look at Frey and find her already staring back. Suddenly, she doesn't look so helpless, demanding protection. When it comes to taking her father down, she's an equal partner, ready for anything. In the end, I don't really have a choice. Still, I say, "We do this together."

"Together," she agrees with a sweet smile that takes my breath away.

Though, it is a task that seems easier said than done, all things considered.

But with her by my side, I feel stronger than I ever have—able to take on anything.

Silas.

Heywood.

The Devil himself.

As long as I have her, we could destroy anyone.

TWENTY-THREE

FREY

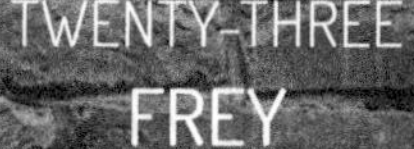

I AM NOT AFRAID. For once, telling myself that doesn't feel like some shallow mantra. At the prospect of facing my father and potentially getting caught in the aftermath of his scheme, death isn't what I fear.

It's losing Daze. It's letting him down. It's proving once and for all that I'm some stupid little girl unworthy of anything but pity.

I'm not afraid as much as I am worried sick, but love has a strange way of making you feel strong against any force that might threaten it. Now that it's out in the open, I feel as though nothing has changed.

And yet everything has.

When our fingers entwine, it feels so natural. As easy as breathing. Perfect. At the same time, it's like being connected to him electrifies me, sending a current of strength through my system. I feel like together we can take on anything.

Whether we actually can or not remains to be seen.

"We'll head to the news station," Daze explains to the others. "You guys start tracking down those locations—we need to find the detonator—"

"And what if Silas shows up as expected?" Damien interrupts. "Or, what if one of those places is rigged to blow?"

"We'll handle it somehow. I guess that's where Lex and his expertise comes in," Daze says darkly, his jaw clenched. I know that look. He's thinking of all the twisted things Silas has done—and whatever he is planning to do still. He intends to make him pay for every last bruise, insult, and indiscretion.

No matter the ultimate cost.

"We'll do our best to handle the explosives," a man with bright auburn hair says. I think Daze called him Damien. "Then we'll converge on your position."

"And if you can't, I want you all to get as far from the city as you can. Ben, you take care of Sam for me, okay?"

Ben rolls his eyes. "Daze, you'll take care of him your damn self because we're all getting out of this alive. Now, enough of the fucking mush mouth shit. Let's get going."

He, Daze, and Damien share a wild, tooth-bared grin. On the surface, they may seem like reckless daredevils itching for violence, but I can tell that beneath the veneer, each and every one of them is aware of what is on the line.

And they're willing to risk their lives.

No one can judge them for that.

TWENTY-FOUR

DAZE

WHEN IT COMES to getting me and Frey downtown quickly enough to intervene in Heywood's speech, the only logical method is to go on foot. With traffic being heavily monitored in and out of the city, stealth is the only option.

While the threat of a clock ticking down toward an imminent explosion looms overhead, I can't deny an unexpected benefit to traipsing through alleyways with Frey by my side.

It's fucking fun. No drug on earth can get you higher than this. Hell, watching her eyes narrow with stern focus is almost better than catching her wide-eyed reactions to pleasure during sex. She's in her element here, keeping pace with every step I take—but with far more confidence than she did, trailing after me like a lost puppy. Gone is the frightened woman she was weeks ago. She walks in lockstep with me, a true partner in every aspect. Rather than fearful and downcast, she holds her head held high as we scope out the fastest route to the news station, and I can't take my fucking eyes off her. Even with a hood drawn low, she's mesmerizing.

"I think I could get used to some more dominant role play when this is all over," I tell her.

She flashes me a smile that makes my dick harden in a heartbeat. "Easy there, tiger. We have to survive today first."

She's damn right about that. While moving on foot is certainly faster than a car would have been, the city is swarming with both people and police. We have to move quickly while blending in with the boisterous foot traffic who have no fucking idea what potentially lies beneath them just a few blocks away.

When we finally make it to the station one more hurdle in our way appears.

"Shit," I tell her. "The security is tight. Seems like your daddy might have had a heads-up about our arrival."

"I don't think so." She's frowning, using that beautiful brain of hers. "It has to be more than a hunch if they have this many officers here and not at city hall."

We watch the patrols for a while, and then something stands out to me.

"They're looking for someone," I say. "Seems like Jamie must have ruffled some feathers. They're on standby for him."

"How are we going to get in?" Frey asks.

"You leave that to me." I scan the building again and hunt for an easy entrance. There isn't one. The police presence is tight, and they're clustered at the building. "We could try to cause a distraction," I say. "I'll draw them away while you head in—"

"That could work," an unfamiliar voice pitches in. "If you want to get shot before you can even get closer, that is. If I've noticed you two, it's only a matter of time before they do."

I whirl around to find a figure dressed in a black hoodie with the hood drawn low. Frey must recognize him because her eyes widen.

"Jamie?"

"I thought you could use some help," he says.

"Well, since they're looking for us both, I don't see another way to get her inside without drawing notice," I point out.

"You're right," Jamie admits. "There is no way to get her in from here. They have the whole entire building surrounded."

"How then?"

He smirks. "We go underground. This way."

He heads for the alleyway we came through and then herds us down a block in the direction opposite the station. After picking his way past a brick building with its windows boarded, he pries open a metal fire door and gestures for us to head inside.

The "inside" being a dark metal staircase leading down.

"If this is some kind of trap, you won't live to tell about it, I can assure you of that," I warn.

Jamie winks. "If this is a trap, then I think we'd all three be dead, and I kind of like living. Come on."

We head into the darkness and reach a small, enclosed landing at the bottom of the steps. There, through another metal door, is what looks like some old maintenance tunnel cutting underground.

"Not many people know about this," Jamie explains while leading the way forward, using his cell phone as a makeshift flashlight. "But it's a shortcut that I discovered from my old coworker."

Abruptly, he turns to a rusted door. "This is the way in, and it'll bring you up the service stairwell. Make a right at the third floor and you'll be within striking distance of the broadcast room."

"And what will we do from there?"

"I'll jam the systems and allow her to broadcast," he says. "She'll be doing the talking, but your job? Clear the way for us to get on air, preferably without getting shot in the process."

"Deal."

"Well, what are we waiting for?" Jamie asks. "It's showtime."

TWENTY-FIVE

FREY

WE MAKE it into the building itself with no trouble, and it's a surprisingly uneventful climb to the third floor. In fact, with its open floor plan and modern design, it's a rather refreshing change of scenery from the small cabin by the lake. It's only when we emerge from the stairwell that the first sign of trouble rears its head.

Namely, in the form of an armed guard standing near a doorway.

"We need to get into that room," Jamie explains. "The longer we can keep from drawing notice of the backup outside, the easier it will be. If I can get access to the security mainframe, I can at least lock the doors and trigger a shutdown. That will slow them down for an hour at least."

"What about getting these people out?" I ask.

Daze smiles in a beautifully dangerous way. "Leave it to me."

I feel my stomach twist, fearing that he intends to do so through violent means. Then I shake myself and remember that Daze isn't like Silas. A fact that he proves in one fell swoop by reaching for a fire alarm button that I didn't even notice.

Just like that, the building erupts into motion as everyone starts to file outside, grumbling in annoyance.

"That was almost too easy," Jamie remarks from our position in a maintenance closet. "But it looks like our friend might need some convincing to play along."

The guard hasn't budged, and he speaks into a walkie-talkie as if coordinating with the officers outside.

"I'll handle this," Daze says. "You two, go do what you need to broadcast."

"This way." Jamie takes my arm and leads me from the room while Daze heads directly toward the guard. All I hear is the sound of flesh connecting with flesh and a startled grunt.

When I look back, Daze is dragging the unconscious guard to a corner of the hallway.

"He'll be fine," he says, meeting my gaze. "Now get in there and make your father's fantasy come crashing down."

Inside the room is a set that dominates most of the open space. Beyond it is a room filled with computers. Jamie races toward one and unloads several items from his bag.

"I can access the security from here, but it will take a while. Maybe you should think about what you want to say?"

It's a question that is surprisingly more complex than I realized before now. I could go on an emotional tirade about my father and what he did to Hale, or the poor people who came to our program for help. I could go on and on about the violence he subjected me to, and how his deceit led to Colton's death. I could even name Silas as his accomplice and go into gory detail about their long reign of terror.

I could tell the horrible truth.

But as Jamie rushes to secure the room and ready the cameras, a new line of conversation comes to mind. I want to talk about this city and why, ridden with crime or not, it doesn't deserve to be destroyed.

It is possible to find beauty even in the most sinful, corrupted things.

DAZE

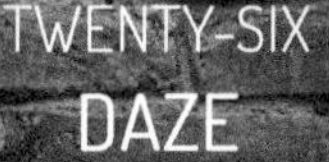

I FEEL like I'm running blind as I guard the door and wait for the broadcast to start. Judging from the state of the place, most of the reporters were already out, covering Heywood's speech from the sidelines. Lucky them.

At least they can look forward to one hell of a spike in ratings—no matter the outcome of the next few hours. Either Heywood gets his due or...

I don't want to think about it. Even with her in the next room, I feel like Frey might as well be on another planet. I'm the only person saving her from any enemies who might barge in—and that's ignoring the fact that this entire room could blow. Somehow, I manage to grab my cell phone and fumble through my contacts list. When I get Damien on the line, the first question out of my mouth is, "Did you find the detonator?"

"Not yet," he replies, sounding as cool as ever. "Three spots down, one more to go."

Which doesn't sound promising in the fucking slightest.

"We have what? Ten fucking minutes?" I ask.

"Nine," he corrects with a dry laugh. "But don't you worry your little head about that. I've got it. Just focus on your girl, and I'll handle things on this end."

"And what if it comes up short as well? Fuck, what if we missed something?"

My stomach sinks at the thought. This whole plan—and Frey's wild gamble—could be for nothing.

"Don't worry," Damien says as if sensing my doubt. "Lex is pretty sure it has to be within the area on the map. He's *rarely* wrong. It's just taking a little longer than expected. Luckily, it seems like the party hasn't started yet—"

"Fuck." Suddenly, one potential location hits me, and I feel ice wash over me. "What if I'm standing right over the first point meant to go?"

It would make sense. Take out the broadcast so that Heywood's speech at city hall is all that remains on air. Which means that Frey could be walking right into his trap.

Or...

"If we are, how can I tell?" I spit out. "I can find the detonator myself, we can end this shit show before it ever begins. Tell me what to look for."

"Hmmm. I'll put on Lex."

There's a rush of air, and a new voice comes through the receiver. "Okay. You're going to look for a small device," the man says. "It will need to be somewhere on the first floor, close to the site of the explosives."

I hiss through clenched teeth. "Sounds easy enough. Anything else? Will it have red blinking lights or some shit?"

"No," Lex says. "It could be anything resembling an electronic device. Something that seems out of place and yet mundane enough to be overlooked. Keep me on the line. I'll try to walk you through it."

"Fine." I take off and scour the empty lobby, feeling my heart pound in my chest. Talk about a twisted game of hide and seek. Ironically enough, I always sucked at the game as a kid.

Fuck me.

"An electronic device," I repeat while scanning at least a dozen television monitors mounted on the wall above the front desk. "I don't know if you've ever been in a news station before, but electronics are kind of a dime a dozen around this place. Can you give me any fucking more than that?"

He pauses. "Well, if you were to blow up a building, where would you hide the detonator?"

I scoff at the question. Then, I think again and scour the room. My eyes land on a cell phone lying on a desk—an odd thing for someone to leave behind. Especially in today's day and age.

One could say it's downright odd.

"Alright, so what if I find it," I blurt while inching toward the device. "What the hell do I do next?"

"Well, you'll need to sever the connection to any potential broadcast signal. Normally, that would mean hacking into it or disrupting the wiring or—"

"Give me the fucking shorthand version for dummies."

"Submerge it in water," he says. "Now!"

Fuck. I hesitate for a second before snatching up the phone and tossing it into a nearby coffee pot, filled to the brim with fresh brew. I don't know if I'm expecting fireworks or what, but with a sad, *thunk,* the device hits the bottom of the glass. Whether or not it'll work, who the fuck knows. Maybe we'll go up in flames. Maybe not.

"We have five minutes to know if you were right or not," Lex says, sounding almost cheerful at the prospect. "But it looks like your girl has made the airwaves, at least. We'll secure the remaining location and then meet you there."

"Good. Because—"

Pain rips through my chest before I hear an explosive pop to accompany it. Not a bomb.

But a gunshot.

My ears ring with the sound. I recognize it instantly—but I barely have time to register the shock. It's as if the world trips into slow motion. As if moving through quicksand, I wind up on my knees, staring at the assailant I didn't even fucking see.

Head cocked, arm extended, he smiles, too damn busy gloating to even utter a greeting. Silas.

TWENTY-SEVEN

FREY

LIGHTS, camera, and action.

Father craved the spotlight, but now that I find myself stepping into the limelight, I don't feel the same thrill. Instead, my words tumble out of me, stammered and hesitant. Gosh, I feel like a high school student again, forced to give a speech in front of the whole class.

Or, in this case, the whole world.

In comparison, my voice barely rises above a whisper, but as the seconds tick by, the nerves diminish. The things I say start to sound more and more assured. Confident. In a trembling voice, I lay out everything, from Hale's death to my father's grand plans for the city. Even I can admit that it sounds insane, and when I finally get the signal from Jamie to stop, I don't know how I feel.

Perhaps, despite everything, I feel stupid. Who would believe me over a powerful politician with so much to lose?

I don't know.

But, I know enough to savor the small miracles when they occur. If the building was due to explode, then it should have happened already. Right? What that means for us, exactly? I'm not sure, but as Jamie flashes a thumbs-up, I hope it's a good sign.

"Okay. That's a wrap," he says next, rising from his computer. "Our signal's been jammed, but I think we did our part here. Besides, we probably have about five minutes before the SWAT team comes bursting in. I don't know where your boyfriend's gone off to, though."

I follow his gaze to the door. Daze isn't in the hallway. My heart sinks. There are only a handful of reasons I can think of for why he might leave.

None of them good.

I rush to the door and don't find him near the stairwell, either. "Where did he—"

A loud sound cuts me off, coming from below. My heart sinks as I recognize it instantly—a gunshot.

"Oh, fuck," Jamie mutters. "We should be careful—wait!"

I barely hear him. I'm already taking off through the double doors and tearing down the stairs. Besides that gunshot, nothing else fazes me. No shouting. No fighting. Nothing.

Daze...

Desperation to find him consumes me to the point that, as I round the counter and race into the lobby, I don't realize what I'm seeing at first. My eyes latch onto Daze first, slumped against the front desk with his left leg outstretched. Thank God, his eyes are open—he's alive. I rush forward only to stop short as my eyes process another chilling component of the scene before me.

Standing beside Daze, casually holding a gun to his head, is Silas.

"You have perfect timing," he says, spotting me with a rabid smile. He looks dressed to kill—literally. The black leather jacket and dark-wash jeans seem tailored to blend into the shadows. Perfect for fading into the background as the chaos of several booming eruptions rocked the city.

"Princess," he says to me. "I wanted you to watch me blow his brains out, just as promised." He adjusts his grip on the gun, and I swear my heart stops beating. My mind flashes ahead, visualizing Daze dead and broken. I move fully on autopilot when I step forward, drawing Silas' notice, but my voice is surprisingly clear.

"Wait. That wasn't all you promised."

"Oh, is that so?" Silas smirks. "What am I missing?"

"Frey, don't," Daze warns, his voice tight. Pained. "Just get the fuck out of here—"

"You promised that you'd make him recount what happened to Renna," I say. "In excruciating detail is how I think you put it."

"Ah…" He bares his teeth. "You're right. But—uh-uh—you can keep your ass right over there!" He aims the gun my way, and I freeze. This isn't the first time I've been faced with such a weapon, but I don't feel the fear that I should. With my focus on Daze, all I can think about is saving his life.

No matter the cost.

"Now, where were we? Oh, right—" Silas kicks Daze hard in his shoulder, leaving him doubled over from the pain. "Tell her all about how you fucked my sister over."

"I cared about Renna," Daze says, his eyes finding mine. "But I didn't love her. I couldn't then."

"And I'm sure you told her that before you knocked her up," Silas snarls, striking Daze with his fist.

"I don't regret being with her, or having Sam," Daze says. "But I won't lie. I know what it feels like to love, and what I felt for her... That wasn't it."

My heart is constricted, and I can barely breathe. Meeting Daze's gaze, somehow, I'm not as afraid as I should be.

"It wouldn't be fair to her to lie," Daze continues, gritting his teeth against the pain. "And I won't do that—"

"Bullshit!" Silas moves to strike him again, and I lunge, grabbing for this hand. For the gun. My heart is pounding in my chest as he easily overpowers me, slamming a hand into my chest, wrenching the gun away—but then I take a page from Daze's book.

I make myself go limp right when Silas tenses to yank me aside. The shift in momentum knocks him off balance, and in a beautiful, fluid motion, Daze rises beside me and snatches the gun from his grasp.

We're at an impasse—a tangled mass of frozen limbs.

Then Daze aims the weapon toward Silas' head and my first instinct is to tell him no.

He can't. Can't...

His finger tenses.

Silas laughs.

I...

I say nothing, even as he finally pulls the trigger.

TWENTY-EIGHT

DAZE

I LET A BULLET FLY, but not where I really want it to strike. Not in Silas' fucking heart, like he deserves—but in his knee. Regardless, he goes down hard, hissing through clenched teeth.

I tighten my grip on the pistol as a metallic taste floods my mouth. I spit on the floor without looking at the color. Could be red. Don't really care.

I'm ready to die just as long as I can take this motherfucker out first. With a howl of pain, he clutches his leg, trying to trap the blood between his fingers.

"That was always the difference between you and me," I choke out, keeping the gun trained on his chest. Then, I change my mind and aim it toward his head instead. "I could handle a bit of pain, but you always pussied out the second there was a risk of getting hurt. You throw out Rena's name, but you want to know something?" My voice deepened at the mere mention of her. I haven't revisited these memories in so damn long. There's no time like the present, though. "That's why she was afraid of you. She knew you'd stop at nothing if it meant protecting yourself. Is that why you had her heroin spiked? Go ahead and deny it."

He grunts, clutching his right leg, forced into a crouch. "You...son of a bitch—"

"And you're a monster who sold out your own damn sister," I snarl. "You know what, Silas? The merciful thing to do would be to put a bullet in your brain, so I don't think I will. I want you to spend the rest of your life stewing in a prison cell, knowing damn well that I'm the one who put you there."

Said out loud, those words almost ring true. Almost. But when I think of him potentially getting out on parole or some shit—and hunting down Frey or Sammy—my finger begins to tighten over the trigger. Not even a heartbeat later, I feel a small hand graze my forearm as a gentle voice enters my ear.

"Daze, don't do this."

Damn. I can't even look at her. Not like this. Instead, I keep my gaze on Silas and consider how fucking good it would feel to put a bullet in between those smug fucking eyes. Even now, he's cocky as hell.

"You think this is funny?" I hit the bastard full in the face with my opposite hand. Blood flies from his mouth, but he's chuckling as he swipes it away.

"What's funny...is that you think you have all the answers, right? But you don't. You fucking idiot." He laughs louder, cocking his head to meet my gaze directly. "You still don't get it, do you? You've already lost? You think this little stunt is gonna do shit?" He looks around and flashes a bloodied grin. "You forget who owns the fucking police. Ah, speak of the devil—"

"Daze!" Frey tugs on my arm, and I finally face her. The expression contorting that slim mouth is the last fucking thing on earth I want to see. She looks horrified. Because of me.

"I'm sorry..." I reach for her, only to stop short, when I realize my knuckles are streaked with blood. But that doesn't seem to be the source of her fear. It just keeps growing by the second. God, it's like she's staring at a stranger. Someone from a nightmare.

"Frey—"

"Daze, oh god, you're bleeding!" She takes my shoulder and tries to steer me closer to the front desk. "You need to sit down."

"I'm fine." I shrug her off without taking my eyes off Silas. The bastard is still chuckling, but he doesn't even try to stand up. Why? He isn't one to surrender lightly. He's up to something. My mind buzzes as I try to consider just what that might be. My ears are ringing. As far as pain goes, I don't feel a damn thing.

But the world sure is starting to fucking sway a hell of a lot.

"What are you planning?" I demand, raising the gun to his skull. "Tell me!"

"Police! Everyone down on the ground!"

Shit. I didn't even hear the bastards come in, but they swarm into the room, dressed head-to-toe in SWAT gear, shields and all. My only coherent thought is to step in front of Frey. I can hear her frantic breaths trickling into my ear. Seems like she's had the same grim realization I have. For all we know, these bastards are on her father's payroll.

And we're caught in the perfect trap.

And suddenly, Silas' taunts make perfect fucking sense. We haven't won. The corruption is too damn deep to ever overcome with a thwarted bombing and a hijacked news conference. I should have known better.

Oh well. "Listen to me," I say to Frey as she starts to comply with the demands shouted at us from every direction.

"ON YOUR KNEES. HANDS UP. DROP THE WEAPON."

"I'll distract them, and you run, you hear me? We can't trust anyone, not even them. Understand?"

"Daze, you're bleeding. You need a hospital—"

"All I need...is you safe." No matter what it takes. Even if it means taking on a room of SWAT bastards.

Even if it means silencing Silas forever.

Even if it means letting her go.

I'm ready for anything.

Except for the world to go black before I can even raise the gun in my grasp.

TWENTY-NINE

FREY

ALL I CAN HEAR IS myself screaming. A sea of faceless individuals shout at me, but I only know they do so from their gaping, soundless mouths. It's a moment eerily similar to the hazy moments when I stood on the edge of a bridge and watched the world pass me by. Present but not aware.

The old Frey was like that—a quiet, meek onlooker in her own life, a slave to the whims of others around her.

Daze changed that. With his gruff demeanor and honest words, he snapped me out of my self-pitying behavior. Gave me a will to fight. Helped me find my backbone.

I can repay that debt by standing still and watching him die.

"Wait!" I issue the shout, and it's as though whoever is in control of the universe hit a fast-forward button. A million things seem to happen all at once.

The police agents move in, still commanding their shouts. I

think some of them even go for their weapons. Doesn't matter. There isn't even time to care about myself.

I step forward, hooking my arms around Daze the second his legs give out. He's so heavy. All I can do is crouch to slow his descent and pray he's merely unconscious. Sensing Silas moving nearby, I have the presence of mind to grab the gun, at least.

Then I just shout out orders without really hearing myself speak. In reality, none of these men should give a damn about anything I say. If they're truly under my father's payroll, all they should do is press a gun to my head and order me into the back of a squad car.

For all I know, that is exactly what happens.

But maybe it's pity on their part or sheer stubbornness on my behalf, but I get them to call an ambulance for Daze first. I make sure to watch him be loaded into the back of it, strapped to a stretcher.

I do that much for him, at least.

I make sure he's alive until the paramedics finally pull off. How long will he be with my father's informants on his payroll is another question entirely.

I'm seated in a darkened room with only a metal table in the center and two chairs. A single light fixture in the ceiling, casts a harsh, artificial glow that is reminiscent of the clinical air of a doctor's office. Nothing about this place instills a sense of care or comfort, however. The walls are a blank, empty gray, but I'm not fooled.

One of them more than likely sports a two-way mirror from behind which an army of officers are probably watching me right now. Along with my father for all I know. Dread builds in my stomach as I think of Daze and everything he's been through already because of me.

Could I have just led him into one last and final trap?

No. I steel myself with a forced inhale and wait. As the seconds tick by, I decide that sitting here patiently serves no one, certainly not me.

"I'm ready to talk," I say out loud while eyeing every inch of this narrow room. "The question is, are any of you really open to hearing the truth? Or is my father's money enough to buy your silence even now—"

The door opens, and a blond man steps inside. I don't recognize him, but I can tell from his demeanor that he isn't from around here. He isn't overly cocky, for one, and as he approaches the table where I sit, he inclines his head respectfully toward me.

"Ms. Heywood? My name is Agent—"

"Respectfully, I don't care what your name is," I blurt out. Where the hell did this newfound attitude come from? Maybe it's simply born out of fear. The longer I stay in here, is more time that Daze is left alone. At risk. They probably took him to the same hospital they took Silas to.

Who's to say my father and his connections haven't already gotten to him?

"I can see that your brother was right to entrust his suspicions to you. I'm assuming he is why you pulled such a brazen stunt earlier, hijacking your father's planned broadcast?"

I stiffen instantly at the mention of Hale. Could it be a trick? A way to taunt me before an inevitable defeat?

Deciding to play it safe, I say nothing. As the seconds tick by, the man continues to watch me, his gaze unreadable. Finally, he sighs and flattens the palm of one hand against the table, inches from my own.

"Well, I can see that we're both ready to cut to the chase," he says. "I'm from the Department of Homeland Security, and all I need from you is one thing. A yes or no answer."

"What's that?"

"To complete my investigation, I need your father on record confirming some of the accusations against him. The only one I can foresee getting anywhere is you. Are you up to that task?"

I can't nod quickly enough, but the words that fly out of my mouth next isn't the polite agreement the old Frey Heywood might issue. Instead, I sound more like... Daze.

A fact I proudly embrace.

"You're damn right I am," I say. "Just tell me when."

THEY SHOW me to another room, but it isn't empty. Someone else sits at the long table identical to the one I'd been handcuffed to moments ago. Beside him is a stern-faced figure that I assume to be a lawyer. It's ironic. My father spent so long deeming himself to be the highest authority in Westpoint City, yet even he knows when to defer to another when facing police interrogation.

When he sees me, his eyes narrow. I can't help the instinctive twinge that makes me wince at the sight of him. My father, the all-powerful leader who ruled my entire life with an iron fist. How diminished he seems now. Still the same man, but somehow smaller in this enclosed space. When he speaks, even his voice sounds different. Gone is the resonating tenor. In its place is a rasping shadow.

"Is this the cause of all this?" he wonders. "The word of my mentally-ill daughter?"

"So you don't deny the charges?" I spit out. My pulse is racing. I can barely sit still, and yet fear isn't the reason for the newfound adrenaline coursing through my veins. It's triumph. To fulfill the agent's request, all I have to do is keep my cool.

And let him do all the talking.

"No one would believe a word coming out of your mouth," my father counters. A muscle in his jaw twitches. A subtle but promising sign. "This is ridiculous—"

"Ridiculous. Like your lies about Hale's death? I know the truth," I insist. "You can't deny it now, and it doesn't matter. You know, I used to admire you and your skill for leadership. I thought that bending others to your will was your strength. But Hale saw through you, right from the start. He always had."

"Your brother was a worthless addict, Frances. I can't be blamed for his failings any more than I could be blamed for yours."

I don't react to the statement right away. Instead, I take the time to settle into the moment and embrace every aspect of it. Some of what I feel is pain—there is no denying it. I look into the eyes of my father, and I can't see the person I once admired more than anyone else in the world. That person is gone, if he ever existed in the first place.

Now, with the remnants of the horror I've lived through on my mind, I have no more delusions about just who I'm dealing with. A monster.

"He was an addict because of you. The heroine you shoved into his veins. We both know it," I finally say, chewing over the words. It's ironic in so many ways that he would choose that word to throw in my face now. Addict.

But he reacts to it. A barely perceptible twitch of his lower lip. Perhaps the start of a denial?

Instead, he laughs. "You are a fool. Your brother was the one who chased a high rather than live up to our family's legacy. The word of a mentally-disturbed woman isn't proof of anything."

He sounds so smug. So confident.

"Then you don't have anything to fear when these agents go through Hale's journal and compare everything in it to the allegations against you," I say, surprised by how damn calm I sound.

And for once—just one brief second—I can see my father's bravado falter. His eyes narrow ever so slightly. Am I telling the truth? He doesn't know.

And when it comes to Michael Heywood, his ego is his main weakness. Always has been.

"And whatever they find will lead back to that criminal Silas and those thugs of his. Not me."

Experience dealing with my father in this arena pays off. I spot a small tell that I doubt I would have noticed before this whole mess started. Back when I was just stupid, innocent Frey so focused on herself and her own pain she was blind to the rest of the world. I'm not that girl anymore, and a twisting sensation in my gut warns me not to let this topic pass. He reacted to it for a reason.

If Daze were here with me, I know exactly what he'd say, "Press the bastard."

So I do. "The truth is, you have no idea what Hale knew. He wrote down every bit of what he'd discovered. Every detail about your secret deal with a heroine dealer. Silas won't take the fall for this. You will—"

"Enough," he snaps, slamming his hands onto the table. "Get her out of here—"

He waves for a guard, but I lunge from my seat, bringing my face within inches of his. Perhaps it's a stupid, reckless move. Maybe I've internalized more of Daze's impulsive bravery than I'd thought. Either way, I feel like a dog with a bone.

If this agent needs cold, hard proof via confession, then that's what I'll give him.

"And," I say to my father's startled expression. "Hale knew all about where you'd stored the illicit goods. These men are just toying with you, Father. They already have a map with the locations circled."

Blue eyes flashing, Michael Heywood looks at me and smirks —but his eyes betray anything but smugness. "Colton Abernathy has his name on those accounts. Not me. He came to me for assistance. Your wayward husband had debts to pay off, Frances. Why else do you think I took pity on him by agreeing to your marriage? Out of respect."

My heartbeat surges through my eardrums. I can barely see straight. Yet, fear isn't the reason.

Just more of that intoxicating sense of triumph.

"We're done here," I say, rising to my feet. I have no idea how I manage to keep my expression neutral, let alone my voice. "Thank you for confirming that aspect of your madness. If they search under Colton's name, they'll find the properties and I'm sure there will be more evidence there tying you both to this mess. By the way..." I turn back to face him. "Did you know that Hale was contacting Homeland Security and feeding them information every step of the way? That's what he was trying to tell me all this time. But that's not what I wanted to tell you. It's this—my mother saw through you, so did Hale, and so did I. Now the entire world knows who you are, but I won't stand here and give you any more of my attention or time."

I turn on my heel and hear him shout after me.

I just keep walking.

THIRTY-ONE

DAZE

MAYBE IT'S the days of accumulated brain damage talking, but, as I come to, I feel like utter shit. Shit, that got scraped off the bottom of someone's shoe. Physically my entire body is fucked—my skull feels shattered, eyes won't open, chest is on fire. The funny thing is that I've endured far worse.

Even the time I nearly got thrown into prison can't compare to now. Because back then, there wasn't a soft, slim hand holding onto my own, or a sweet voice whispering into my ear as though its owner had nothing but time in the world to sit at my side.

"Daze, please wake up."

I'd stay in a coma forever if it meant keeping her here, safe from harm. Safe from the entire fucking world. But then her other hand must settle over my chest because it hurts like hell.

"Shit," I croak, peeling my eyes open. "Be gentle with the merchandise, baby."

She laughs at me, but it isn't one of those fake ones she'd gotten so good at putting on in her life as a rich, preacher's daughter. It's real, with her head thrown back to display her thin throat. Politely, she looks like hell, still covered in dried blood. Her hair is a mess, but the smile shaping that pink mouth is even more genuine than her laughter is.

"I take it, your father's men aren't standing outside, waiting to put a bullet in my skull?"

"No." Her smile widens, and she's more beautiful than ever. "We won't have to worry about him for a while. At least until a trial—"

"Sounds like you've been busy."

"No, but my father was," she counters, her mouth twisted in a frown. "Turns out, he had his sights set beyond Westpoint City, and he was willing to make a deal with the devil to achieve it. A cartel, in this case. A man who dabbles in human trafficking and sacrifices to uphold his mystique. My father entertained him. Maybe he even believed in it, who knows." Her eyes well up though she does her best to blink any tears back.

"Hey." I reach out despite the throbbing pain extending my arm triggers. Gently, I rap my knuckles against her cheek, avoiding the still-healing bruises. When she looks at me, I raise my voice to ensure she can't ignore a single word. "He's not your responsibility. Never was. You didn't choose to be his daughter, but when it came down to obeying him blindly or doing the right thing... You made that choice. No one else. That took guts."

She nods solemnly. "At least now I know that Hale didn't die for nothing. It was his tip that triggered a higher investigation. Without his journal, none of this would make any sense."

"His death was never in vain," I point out, raising her hand to my mouth. I run my lips along the knuckles of her fingers, registering the new scrapes and scars marring the pale flesh. "He always had you. He knew you'd fight for him, and you have."

"But now what?" she asks, her voice soft, eyes lowered. "I don't have Hale to fight for or my father to rebel against. What do I have left?"

I chuckle, sensing where this line of questioning is headed. In any case, I'm more than eager to supply the right answer. "And now," I say, "you have me."

Her upper lip quirks. "You're damn right I do. And..." She leans in, letting her warm breath fan over my jawline. "I wouldn't have it any other way."

It's done. Happily fucking ever after. Right?

Not quite. A week later, and while Heywood's little speech may have ended with him in cuffs, I know it's not over yet. Who the hell knows if either he or Silas will try to get a foothold in the city again.

For now, the motherfucker is contained, and that's good enough for me.

I can't say the same for Silas. Shooting the bastard was cathartic, I won't lie—but I can't explain what made me aim for his leg and not for his head. Maybe age has made me a soft motherfucker.

In any case, Silas will recover soon enough, but he won't have a crew to lead anymore. The newly-restored Saints will see to that. I'll see to that. Besides, with a long stint in prison likely in his near future, he won't have the chance to mount any plan for revenge.

As for Frey...

I watch her, spinning in a circle with Sammy on her hip. He laughs and squeals, having a blast. The smile on her face isn't wide or ecstatic—but it's something. It will take time to recover from the shit she's been through.

After telling her story to the feds, she's had to watch her father be thrown in prison and learned that her stepmother's body was found in the remnants of the Abernathy compound. Not just her, but Colton, and an unidentified female—proof of her horror story and more than enough to take down the entire ring her father entertained. While the main Abernathy mansion lies in ashes, the feds were able to find an underground compound beneath their fancy family estate ripe for drug trafficking to and out of Westpoint. Not ironclad evidence exactly, but suitable enough to keep El Diablo and his goons from the city for a while at least.

Beggars can't be choosers.

In any case, the files we stole from Silas will be the proverbial nail in the coffin for both him and Heywood, but I don't feel like gloating about it. Go figure.

I just want to watch her. Linger in her presence.

No matter what happens or what comes next.

I'm never letting her go.

THIRTY-TWO

FREY

ISN'T it funny how your life can turn out differently than you imagined? As a young girl, I believed that a knight in shining armor would win my heart, like in my favorite fairy tales. Thinking back on it now is like observing the fantasy of a complete stranger. Particularly since my reality turned out to be totally different.

In society's eyes, Daze Keaton, a biker with an extensive record, isn't the ideal hero. This is a savior no woman should idolize, let alone a preacher's daughter.

But he is all I want—a perfect, wild devil.

I go over to him and set Sammy down. Giggling, he races inside to get a toy, and I take advantage of the brief moment of quiet to slip my hands around Daze's shoulders.

He watches me, a blond eyebrow raised, his gray eyes sparkling in the sunlight.

This moment feels so surreal. Not too long ago, I would cringe from this man if I saw him walking down the street.

And now?

I can't imagine life without him.

"What are you thinking?" he wonders as his mouth forms a dangerous half-smile.

I dwell on the answer in silence. Then I stand on tiptoe and press my lips against the hard line of his jaw. "You," I say. "How perfect you are."

He laughs, and my entire body feels warmer than the sunlight alone could ever achieve. "Liar. You're thinking about how you're going to dump me for a prince or some shit now that you're a millionaire."

I wince even though I know he's joking. The irony is, at least part of that statement was the cold, hard truth—as it turns out, my father put all his illegal dealings in my mother's name. Beneath the swagger and bravado, he was broke, on the edge of a financial cliff. Marrying me off to Colton was more than a chauvinistic show of pride.

He was counting on access to the Abernathy fortune before he could secure his right to my mother's estate.

And now...

Somehow, everything he wanted is now mine. Every dime he'd stolen from my mother's estate. All her inheritance, including stocks and property.

Not that I want it. The thought makes me sick. All of it is tainted with blood. Daze's warm smile reveals that he knows exactly what I'm thinking.

"You aren't them, Frey," he says, reaching up to brush his thumb along my cheek. I lean into the caress, and he indulges me, keeping his hand there, imparting a steady warmth. "You're going to use this money in a way Hale and your mother can be proud of."

"And Catherine," I add, recalling her final words to me. "I owe them that much."

Daze nods. "You're right," he murmurs. "But, in between all that do-gooding, I have some ideas as to what we can do when you aren't trying to save the world."

"Is that so?" I counter, raising an eyebrow. A flicker of movement draws my attention as, behind him, Sammy races into view, brandishing a toy firetruck. "I think I may have some compelling competition for your time."

As if on cue, Sammy pipes up, "Daddy, look! I got this! See?"

Daze isn't even fazed as he flashes Sam a warm smile while tilting his body into me. "You should know by now that I'm man enough to go around."

"So what did you have in mind?" I ask.

Daze steps back from me, flashing a mocking wink. "Something too X-rated to say in current company."

He turns to Sammy and lifts him into the air, spinning him around while he laughs.

And I couldn't imagine a better moment than this. We're in this together for better or worse, but I know it won't be all smooth roads up ahead. Rather than hide from my father's legacy, we'll rebuild Salvation from the ground up and make it something worthy of the reputation it unfairly garnered.

And if kindness alone isn't enough, I know a sinner who doesn't mind getting his hands dirty.

ABOUT LANA SKY

Lana Sky is a reclusive writer in the United States who spends most of her time daydreaming about complex male characters and parenting her Cockapoo Joey. She writes dark, twisted romance across several genres. Her titles include everything from mafia romance to vampires.

facebook.com/AuthorLanaSky

x.com/lanasky101

amazon.com/author/lanasky

pinterest.com/lanasky101

goodreads.com/lanasky

instagram.com/lanasky101

bookbub.com/authors/lana-sky

tiktok.com/@author_lana_sky

ALSO BY LANA SKY

For more titles by Lana Sky, please visit:

https://www.lanaskybooks.com